I0557706

On The
Backs of Donkeys

Elaine Watkins

Absolute Author
Publishing House

Published by Absolute Author Publishing House

ISBN – 978-1-64953-272-5

Illustrations by Julia Day
Book Design by Aubree Lawson

Printed in the United States of America

For Deyon and Dez

Acknowledgments

Thank you to the Taunton writers group. Bernadette Norton, Jen Fahey, Joe Perrault, Bree Berube, Nita Iracks, and Rita Ouellette, your comments, suggestions, and support were valuable during the evolution of this book.

My donkeys would not have had a consistent voice if not for Robin Weidner. I'm grateful for the time she gave my book in its early stages.

My readers, Bobbye Trotter, Darcy Costa and Bree Berube were instrumental in helping me to see new possibilities that led to important changes. A special thanks to Jen Fahey, a wonderful writer and minister, for her incisive reviews that helped me add layers to my characters.

I'm extremely grateful for the partnership of Julia Day (Luz), who enlivened my words with her art. Her insightful depictions embodied the spirit of the boys and donkeys. Her whole-hearted eagerness renewed my energy for this story.

Without my dear friend Judy, I would not have gotten the donkey out of the barn. Her generosity and unwavering belief in me moved the project and moved my heart.

And not least in any way, I was spurred on by my sisters in blood and by graft. Shirley Watkins, Valerie Harper, Marilyn Virgil and Jean Noyes have been a wonderful cheering section, a wind at my back.

Praise for
On the Backs of Donkeys

"Elaine Watkins writes a deeply moving story, full of biblical symbolism and meaning that touches the depth of human experience and emotion. While reading, I laughed, cried, turned the pages quickly to see what was next, and frequently just paused to enjoy a scene or description. Writing in the genre of C.S. Lewis' Chronicles of Narnia, Elaine invites you to ponder your family, relationships, and faith."

Jim McCartney
Author of *Justice, Jesus, and the 21st Century Church, Do You Get It?*

"Elaine Watkins' book, On the Back of Donkeys, draws you in. It is a charming, yet rich and deeply spiritual story of friendship, and purpose that will lead the reader to unexpected self- reflection. I have known Elaine for 25 years and treasure her ability to communicate spiritual truths with a profound understanding of the human condition in all its complexities. Her characters benefit from her insightful wisdom, allowing the reader to quickly connect to their personal struggle and ensuing transformation. A true delight."

Carol McGuirk
Christian Singer/Songwriter, Women's Ministry Leader, Paris, France

"You're in for a treat. This story is a great representation of the power of God and the need for friendship. Elaine has done a masterful job of communicating both of these principals at a very high-level. For young and old this enchanting story is poised to become a classic."

Lloyd Lamarre
Educator, Coach

"An insightful and artistically crafted story of love and the power of relationship...*On the Backs of Donkeys* is a must-read with a message that persists even past the final sentence!"

Bree Berube
Writer, artist

"*On the Backs of Donkeys* opens up chambers of the heart wherein love and acceptance can be both joyful and unsettling. Elaine Watkins explores relationships, both animal and human, and how feelings are sorted out in the quest for belonging. Her book is a poignant, insightful page turner."

Suzette Martinez Standring
Syndicated Spirituality Columnist, GateHouse Media
Award-winning author, speaker, TV show host

"*On the Backs of Donkeys* is a modern Christian tale perfect for any child who has felt 'weird' or left out. The story affirms God's presence amidst the weird ones, the ones holding pieces of broken friendship, and all the others who have felt excluded. It's a great, feel good read that might inspire the reader to pick up their Bible in search of donkeys."

Rev. Dr. Rachael Keefe
Pastor, educator, speaker. Author of *The Lifesaving Church, Barefoot Theology*

"Elaine's voice winds a supernatural story around characters real enough to break your heart. With stunning insights into the human (and animal) spirit, On the Backs of Donkeys is a daring and poetic journey that intrigued my imagination from the first page, and inspired inner strength by the last page. I can't wait to read it again."

Jen Fahey
Award-winning writer, Pastor

"*On the Backs of Donkeys* is a book with intriguing and layered characters and is appropriate for both middle readers and adults. The words sang to me, drawing me in. I couldn't wait to see what happened next. I would have happily read it all in one sitting. This book is fabulous."

Sandra N. James
Graphic Artist

Chapter One

Royce and Chrissy were best pals. It didn't matter that one was a boy and the other a donkey. They skipped about in harmony, their spirits tied together in friendship and mutual understanding. They felt blessed and safe, grateful for the company of the other. The possibility that anything could come between them seemed inconceivable, laughable. But that was before another boy came, riding on a horse.

The donkey, Chrissy, and the boy, Royce, were in their favorite meadow going about the fun and serious business of examining flowers, frogs, and the shape of stones. They took breaks in their doings to replenish their energy, pausing in thankfulness to God before sharing their food feasts. In these particular days, the sun changed its position in the sky and daylight shortened its stay. For now, it still offered the playful sparkling of light, making shapes with leaves and illuminating the flitting, flying things. It warmly caressed their faces, tracing memories for what would soon be over. The time to put aside sunshine activities moved closer.

The boy would also be putting behind his lesson time at home and would attend school with the other eleven year olds. That made the sunshine fun things more fun, but with a funny feeling. It reminded him of those berries that started out sweet at first bite, but had a tart ting at the end.

Father had said, "Royce, the time for carefree boy ways are coming to an end. You'll be carrying more responsibilities soon."

He hadn't said it like it was punishment; but rather, like a privilege. It made Royce want to square his shoulders and walk as tall as he could. He wanted to do the man things. He saw that Father's expression was something like the berries tasted.

Royce was a little skittish, but as long as he had his best friend, Chrissy, he would be just fine. Chrissy always understood him, and he understood her. When she'd first entered the world, Father said, "Her name is Jenny." Royce had tilted his head and said, "No, Father, her name is Chrissy. Father had nodded and given him a look that he couldn't name.

Chrissy and Royce had been companions since her birth. Nothing disturbed their bond until the boy with the horse came to spoil things. The shadow of that other boy and his horse crept up on Royce and Chrissy while they drowsed with sluggish eyelids after their noon meal of carrots, sandwiches, pears, and barley straw.

* * *

The shadow fell over Chrissy, making her shiver, though the day was very warm even in the shade of the trees. Chrissy noticed the eager shine of Royce's eyes af-ter the initial surprise. The new boy's legs hung from his horse, longer and thinner than Royce's. They matched those of his horse which Chrissy looked at warily. Other boys hardly ever came to play with Royce. Occasionally his kin came, urged by the hands of their adults. After a short playtime with Royce, the adults released them to go on to other activities because of what they called Royce's "specialness." Chrissy knew that it made Royce sad, but he had her to soothe him. She moved closer to Royce just in case unkind words were thrown at him. Royce automatically stroked the fur on Chrissy's back.

"Have some carrots and pears," Royce offered to the boy on the horse who'd said nothing beyond the silent language of his bemused perusal of the scene. The mounted boy was quiet for too long. When he did speak, after twisting his mouth to one side, he said, "I don't eat donkey food."

Chrissy saw Royce's skin get deeper, as though the sunset had lent its colors. "I have sandwiches too," he stammered. He snatched his hands back from Chrissy's fur, causing her to shiver again. Chrissy watched as Royce awkwardly got on his knees to rummage among the food remains, coming up with nearly half a sandwich, extending it to the boy.

Giving a snorting laugh, the boy slid from the horse with the grace of water pouring over rocks, "I ate earlier." With the same twist-mouth expression, he flicked his hand in a careless wave, "Put that away."

The sunset color still in his face, Royce jerked back the bread and meat sandwich. The movement caused the roasted beef slice to slip out, landing on the ground. Scrambling around, Royce picked up the meat, finally tucking it slap dash back into the bread.

Meanwhile, the new boy watched with his keen eyes, which Chrissy noticed were a lighter version of the sky; but against the paleness of his skin, they looked dark. "I'm Chadwick," he said, putting out his hand towards Royce. "But call me Chad."

Royce stood again, wiping his mustard-smeared hand on his short trousers, leaving a mark there. "I'm Royce," he said, squaring his shoulders and using a voice a little deeper than usual. He took Chads hand, shaking it too vigorously.

Chad laughed, "I heard that you're starting school again just like me. We can be new together." The smile that filled up his face had the invitation of an oat field. Chrissy could feel the urge to draw closer to him. Even as her head leaned forward, her feet moved backward. It made her think of the yes and no feeling she got around a black widow's web.

"You seem like you'd make a good pal," the boy added.

Chrissy could see the relief that spread into a wide smile on Royce's face. Chrissy brayed a warning without knowing precisely why.

"It's okay, Chrissy. Chad and I will be scared together and not alone."

Chad's face changed to that of clouds before the rains came. "I'm not scared. My dad made me come to be your friend because everyone else thinks you're weird. I was just being nice." He turned away to where his horse was grazing. He didn't leave, though.

"I shouldn't have said out loud that you're scared," Royce said.

Chrissy heard the tight tone to his voice. She knew that Royce had just done that thing that caused him to stay home and others to avoid him. Royce's face had lost the sunset colors and all other colors as well. Chrissy nuzzled into his side.

Chad had his stiffened back towards Chrissy and Royce. He at last turned around with a hint of sparkle in his eyes, "I'll give you another chance." He sat on the ground, his head indicating that Royce should do the same. Royce obeyed the silent command and they sat thus until eventually, Royce's shoulders eased down from his ears and his breaths became longer and deeper.

"If you had a real horse, we could ride together," Chad said.

Chrissy, who had settled next to Royce, lifted her head, letting out another bray to get the attention of the horse. If she made friends with the horse, Chad would see that they could all ride even if she wasn't a horse. She was a sturdy donkey after all. The bray failed to get the job done so she jumped up to move closer. As Chrissy approached, the horse turned its hind quarters towards her with a dismissive swish of her tail.

Chad's sticky spider laughter was harsh on Chrissy's ears. But it didn't hurt as much as the smaller, uneasy laughter from Royce.

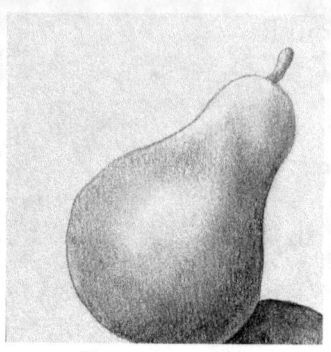

Chapter Two

The changes seemed small at first, and to some, welcome. On the outside looking in, it didn't seem like anything was missing. It seemed like something was added. But Chrissy was on the inside and knew the wrongness. Or maybe the otherness.

At first the four, boys and beasts, enjoyed the meadow and woods together. Royce sat astride Chrissy, loping along while Chad and the horse, Dara, pranced alongside, sometimes taking off at quicker speeds. Chad tossed pitying looks at Royce during such times.

One time, Chad brought pears that were different from the green ones that Chrissy and Royce usually enjoyed. These were red and softer. "I got these especially for you, Chrissy," said Chad, surprising and confusing her. He watched with eager expectancy, waiting for Chrissy to try them.

She watched the corners of his mouth and his shoulders pull down as she ignored them, munching carrots instead. After some moments during which the boys said nothing, Royce picked up two of the pears. One he took a bite of, the other he offered to Chrissy.

"It was nice that Chad brought you a gift. These pears are different, but they're good. Here, take a bite."

Chrissy took a bite, obeying the anxious entreaty in Royce's tone. She took a bite for each bite that Royce took until she had eaten the entire pear. Chad looked on, silent and standing apart; his thin legs seemed to wobble. He eventually sat down with lips pressed tightly as if to keep something from escaping.

A thought landed across Chrissy's mind that she should feel bad that she felt somewhat good about Chad being left out. She quickly shooed it away. She had too much joy that she and Royce were almost sharing lunch together again. The fact that Chad had brought the pears spoiled it just a bit. She admitted to herself that the pears were good, but she kept imagining that she was eating spider webs.

Chrissy and Royce didn't mingle lunches anymore; not since Chad came. Royce took care now to separate their food. It pricked Chrissy like a nettle patch, but she was grateful that Royce did not heed the taunts and cajoling of Chadwick to get a real horse. At least he didn't in the beginning.

One morning in the usual way of things, Chrissy stood waiting at the door for Royce. She looked forward to the early day time of inspecting the world with her boy. It was more precious because their ritual would soon be interrupted by school; but mostly because it was time without Chad and the snobby Dara. Those two often arrived in the meadow when the sun was almost straight above. Those Chad-less times felt almost like they used to.

But even in the absence of Chadwick and Dara, their pending arrival left an impression. After a while, Royce would glance at the time keeper on his wrist or turn his head too many times in the direction that Chad and Dara usually approached. During those instances, Chrissy would bray and prance in a way that mimicked Dara. She had taken to practicing it. It made Royce laugh and look at her, and only her, for just a bit.

But this day, Chrissy stood watching the back door of the house where Royce slept with his family.

The sun travelled to straight above and beyond, but Royce never came. The father came and laid barley grass in reach and offered carrots from his hands, but Chrissy didn't have an appetite. She wondered if Royce had gone away forever like the father's father. Almost always Royce said goodbye and waved his hands when he was going away for a while. And when he was sick, Chrissy could visit with him at his window. Royce always said goodbye.

The father didn't behave like his heart was torn up, so Royce probably didn't go into Forever. He must be sick. That had to be it. Chrissy hurried to the window that she knew to be Royce's sleeping place and brayed loudly, barely stopping to breathe. The father tried to quiet her with shhh sounds and murmurs, and he tried stroking her. Chrissy moved away and continued her desperate appeal.

After a long time of unceasing calls for her boy, Royce rounded the corner of the house. Chrissy stopped mid-bray and made a speedy lope to him. He made soothing sounds, stroked and petted Chrissy. He knelt and Chrissy laid her head on his shoulder. She tried to look in his eyes, but Royce's eyes shirked her glance. He said he was sorry he hadn't said goodbye. Chrissy knew that his words were not all the way true. Royce smelled of Chad and Dara and other horses. Royce poured out words of a party he had gone to. He told about horse rides and other children. His voice was like the rush of running and skipping through grass. He had been included. Chrissy's otherwise happiness for him sat in place alongside the fear that she was not needed or wanted anymore. Royce promised with lots of words that he would remember her the next time. Chrissy had a terrible feeling that his words were not true. And she was right.

* * *

By and by, Chrissy stopped waiting at the door. Sometimes Royce would think of her, but more and more, he would go frolicking without her. He spent the last of the shortening days before school with Chadwick, who always dictated what they were doing even if Royce had other ideas. And Chadwick was mean; sometimes more than other times.

He didn't always bring Dara, coming instead in a big car that he exited, taking slow steps to the porch. Those days he sat and made Royce bring him things, and he didn't want to go to the meadow and the little woods.

One of those days, the day before Royce would start school again, Chrissy dared to join them on the porch, hungry for time with her boy. She laid her head on his lap and he sat cross-legged, ruffling her coat.

"It's like a live stuffed bear," Chad said. "I used to cuddle a teddy bear when I was four. If you're going to school and hanging with me, you can't have teddy bears. That's weird."

The words caused both Chrissy and Royce to stiffen.

"You want me to choose you because you're scar- I mean, you think Chrissy takes too much of my attention," he said.

This time, Chadwick stiffened. Chrissy, confident that Royce would tell the intruding boy to go back where he came from, allowed a satisfied smirk to shape her mouth. They would return to enjoying their pears, barley grass, apples and sandwiches, thanking World-Maker for their bounty, and bond once again over their special understanding.

Chrissy cast a pitying look at Chadwick; she knew what it was like to lose Royce even for a little while. She waited for the pronouncement. Her heart lifted to the height of the eagles as mind pictures played in her head. She would wait for Royce after school. They would do his lessons in the meadow, or the barn when the cold was too much. He would need her again and say he was sorry for the past few weeks. Their bond would be unbreakable.

A yes/no battle disturbed Royce's face. That caused a prickle to Chrissy's heart, but she was mostly certain of the victor. She watched with smug assurance as Royce looked longingly at Chad, who had his own war playing over his face. She saw the moment Royce's face appeared hard and smooth like river stones. Chrissy even managed to be a bit sad over Chad's expected kick in the hide. She couldn't help but think what a good and gracious donkey she was to do that.

When the words came, it took a moment to realize that they were wrong side up from what she expected.

"You're right, Chad. I don't need my donkey anymore. It's kinda dumb to have it as a pet. I'll be going to school and I don't want to look weird. It's time for me to act normal." Royce stood abruptly and Chrissy's head lost the cushion of his lap, meeting the wood planks of the porch with a plunk.

"Go away. shoo!" said Chad. "You belong with the other animals."

"Go Chrissy." Royce gave the command in a voice like ice puddles breaking under foot.

Chrissy froze, with ears full of disbelief. It was Royce's foot giving her a not-so-gentle prod that got her moving in slow motion. Her head felt too heavy to lift and she wanted to be small.

After several dragging steps, she turned to look at Royce in pitiful hope. But he didn't look back. Instead, she saw that he now sat on the porch bench beside Chad, who had draped his thin arm around Royce, their heads close together. Chrissy had wanted to plead to Royce's eyes, but it was Chad that stared at her coldly, squeezing Royce's shoulders in ownership. The usurper quickly looked away, but not before Chrissy saw in his expression a look like the sound of a mourning dove.

* * *

It began to sink in that Chrissy's cast away was real. No Royce showed up to apologize and be pals again. She began to hate her stature, her stolid shape and not-enough-ness. Hope scuttled away, replaced by a pain that settled in her heart. The pain called to mind the time she'd stepped in a gopher hole and injured her leg. Except this was worse. There was no Royce to reassure her with ten-der gentleness that the hurt would go away and that he would be there. The pain spread out over the rest of her.

Chrissy had been forsaken. The misery, foreign and overpowering, filled her, saturating her. It had no place to go except out past her throat and through her mouth. Chrissy let it out in long wretched notes.

15

Chapter Three

Royce couldn't bear the sound. He hadn't known that donkeys could cry. At first, he didn't know what it was – the mournful voice. He'd thought it was a human crying. But when he recognized that part of the sound was like a donkey's bray, he realized that it was unmistakably Chrissy. Tossing on his bed, he covered his head with his pillow against the unrelenting sound. The noise followed him under the comforter, taking over his ears and threatening his heart.

For a moment, or two or three moments, Royce had the urge to throw back his covers, stuff his feet into his slippers, race to the barn, and bury his face against the neck of his pal. He wanted to comfort Chrissy and comfort himself. He longed to get things back to the time before they became complicated.

But the recollection of Chad's disdainful eyes and words mocked this sentiment, preventing his legs from swinging over the side of the bed. It was stupid to be best pals with a beast, he reasoned. He needed a real friend, not a pretend one…. But Chrissy had been like a real friend…. No, maybe all along it had been Royce's imagination that he could understand her…. In that moment, he hoped that he had made it up. Because that imagination felt like blame trying to make him believe that Chrissy's cry was saying, "Why did you leave me? My insides are breaking." Royce's insides felt like breaking too.

The cries were like a pointing finger that he couldn't escape. Perhaps…No! It was just a stupid animal. Besides he had school tomorrow. He tried to conjure up the fear and excitement of that, but Chrissy's clatter intruded. Royce got mad. Chad was right about Chrissy being a nuisance. She was so inconsiderate. He scooched down in his bed, put the pillow over his head again, and drew his comforter over the pillow. He tried to sleep.

* * *

Royce was cranky. At breakfast, his grumpiness drained Mother's good cheer. He posed sullenly as she snapped a picture to mark the occasion of his first day back to public school. She said a special prayer and gave him a pep talk, thinking nervousness was the source of his sour attitude.

"It's going to be fine, and now you have a friend to hang with. You'll see; it won't be bad," she assured. Royce's grunting, bleary-eyed response finally drew a heavy sigh from her. With a shrug and a concerned meeting of eyes with Father, she picked up her briefcase and headed off to work.

Father didn't say anything for a long time. He read the paper while eating sausages and oatmeal topped with bananas and a drizzle of maple syrup – Royce's favorite. When he was loading the dishwasher, he spoke.

"Chrissy misses you."

"Umph," was Royce's unintelligible response as he repositioned the sausage that he had carefully cut in uniform bite-sized pieces.

"You have a big heart," Father continued. "It has a lot of room."

Royce wanted to yell, "Shut up!" as loud as he could. Instead he put on his I-don't-care face. He also imagined building a wall around his heart. That was better, cushioning him from some of his angst, but not good enough to totally block out Chrissy's terrible outpouring of pain.

* * *

Royce would have preferred to start his new school life with a good night's sleep to boost him. As he approached Benedict Academy, memories of the di-sastrous time several years ago when he'd last attend-ed school made war with the echoes of Chrissy's cry-ing. Both intruders shoved for prime position, with the school memories winning out with a sliver of an edge once he arrived at the academy.

A full two minutes passed after Father stopped the car before Royce pushed the door open and put his feet on the pavement. He finally exited at the urging of Father's hand gently on his shoulder. Suddenly, Chad stood in front of him, his eyes looking bigger against his pale skin, a smile taking over his thin face. Royce answered the smile.

As usual, his joy at seeing Chad was tempered by the tight ball of fear and sadness that lived lashed to his friend. Royce knew that he should not mention those things. Chad wouldn't like it. Royce's own fear whispered that Chad wouldn't be his friend anymore if he said anything. He wanted – *needed* – Chad to like him.

He also knew that Chad needed him in a hungry way that made Royce want to make things better for him. He couldn't say anything about that either.

The two boys walked up the steps to the school together. Royce could feel the stares and non-covert looks of his current and former school mates. He kept his eyes looking at the ground or straight ahead. Chad did the opposite; he cheerfully said hello to anyone in their path. Most responded in a like manner.

At the glass door entrance to the school, Royce, in a moment of panic, turned around to see if his father was still there. He was. Father watched him steadily. Royce wanted to turn around and rush back to the safety of the car. Indeed, his feet tried to obey his wish; they made a half turn, his body following.

A hand touched his arm. Royce swiveled and saw that it was Chad. "You can do this, bud," Chad said.

The words were said with confidence, but Royce also saw and felt the panic rising in Chad. He sensed the disturbance of the fear/sad ball inside his friend. He couldn't leave him. And just as well because when he turned back towards the door, reflected there, was the movement of Father's car as it drove away.

There would be no running back to the safety of his meadow or back to the companionship of Chrissy.

The warring factions inside shifted again. Echoes of Chrissy's braying sadness took over, temporarily upstaging his school fears, attaching to him like a pesky swarm of agitated wasps.

* * *

Royce followed Chad inside. On the other side of the glass, students were milling about in careful rambunctiousness. The customary din was a smidge muted in deference to the first day, an almost pause to mark the beginning of something. The scents of new clothing, books, and supplies mingled with that of the polish on the highly glossed floors.

The smell of the floor wax, along with the familiar sounds, sent him back to before. The memories made a knot in Royce's throat, and squeezed his belly. The power of them made his feet heavy and slow. The air from his lungs came out in shorter, quicker bursts. A feeling of being there but not there started to settle over him. That's when he felt a gentle nudge, bringing him back. For a moment he thought it was Chrissy, who used do that to show her caring and support. It wasn't Chrissy, of course. It was Chad's elbow giving him a nonchalant poke as if his arm accidently brushed him in passing. Royce knew better and was grateful.

"Let's find our homeroom," Chad said. He led

the way, walking tall, the slight wobbliness of his legs covered by confident, easy strides.

Arriving at the classroom, Royce watched Chad adopt an open carefree look, tossing a smile here and there at the obviously curious. The carefree wasn't real, but it worked. Once again, kids responded in a positive way. Naturally, there were the side eyes for Royce, but he expected that. One or two gave him a wary hello. Royce's return hello came out in squeaky surprise. Ducking his head, he took a seat beside the one that Chad had chosen.

When students were mostly settled, the teacher gave a fawning introduction of Chad, saying she hoped he would feel welcome in his new town and new school.

"Thank you, Mrs. Thomas," Chad answered. "Everybody has been really nice so far. And Royce and I hung out a lot this summer. So, I already have one good friend. He's sort of new, too. He said the 'too' a little harder than the rest of the words. He tilted his head slightly, giving the teacher an expectant look.

"Oh! Of course, um, we're glad, well, welcome back, Royce. She didn't meet Royce's eyes, but made other of his facial parts her target. Her fingers played nervously on the sleeves of her hopeful looking dress that was bright orange with white daisies.

Chad gave her a smile as if bestowing a doggy treat for good behavior.

"Thank you," Royce said, pressing his lips together. He put a halt to the flow of words that wanted to come out. What was knocking against his lips, but he didn't say was, *'I'm glad you're not drinking too much anymore. And I'm sorry that when I was here before, I asked you why you called yourself Mrs. since you weren't married."*

Those sort of unbridled words were what caused problems before, making him seem weird. Weird and scary, they had said. He felt Ms. - *Mrs.* – Thomas's relief that there were no additional words from him. The rest of the students had watched the exchange with tense anticipation but were disappointed or glad that there was no drama. Their interest shifted.

Truthfully, Royce barely noticed their reaction; he was sinking into the delicious feeling that he had a friend; one who had stood up for him in from of everybody. He pushed aside the pesky wasps that tried to intrude and point out that Chrissy had always had his back.

He did notice one person in the room who worried him a little. Lyda Hoskins. Her white blonde hair was in a ponytail so tight that it must have hurt. Her shirt and jeans were different colors, but they had a rosy tint to them. It reminded him of the time he had mistakenly put a new red towel in with lighter towels. He felt bad because of the why. Her clothes were one thing, but what concerned him was that she was the kind of sad that made her mad. Like Chad, she was pretending. She acted nice, but her nice had knife edges.

Royce felt words piling up in his mouth, urging him to spill them; he swallowed them, catching her eye instead. He tried to communicate understanding and compassion. What he received back was the promise of knives. He jerked at the intensity and quickly looked away. Maybe he could avoid her. But he knew she wanted someone to unload her mad onto. And she had chosen him.

The rest of the school day went better than Royce had feared, but also worse. The previous night's sleeplessness played havoc on his concentration. He pinched himself a few times when he felt his head sinking towards his desk.

The best part of the day was that a lot of kids wanted to be Chad's friend, but he made it clear that Royce was his favorite. Under his friendship protection, Royce didn't become an instant outcast. He could tell that some were wary, but they didn't dare say bad things with Chad there. Hope arose in him that maybe he could have more friends and not be a weirdo loner.

Another good part was that he remembered to keep his mouth shut about certain things.

Except one time.

He was mostly not sorry.

It happened during World History and Chad wasn't there. Lyda Hoskins was. When Royce entered the classroom and saw her sitting towards the front, he sat in the back out of her line of sight. He thought he had escaped her notice, but twenty minutes before the bell, she kept her sharp-edged promise. Royce felt it coming before she spoke, but he was in the middle of a big tonsil exposing yawn and didn't have time to brace himself.

Lyda swiveled around and in a loud voice asked, "Are your kinfolks African gypsies? Were you born with a crystal ball for a brain?" A few kids tittered. "Maybe we should call you ball head." More kids joined the laughter.

It was stupid and childish. It was a deliberately placed burr under saddle-sore skin.

He should have ignored her. But her comment struck a bullseye on Royce's rather round head. His chagrin egged him on to respond with blades of his of his own. A familiar sensation filled him. There was a choice there, but he didn't stop himself. He let the words, tainted by retaliation, rush out.

"You're sad that your mother went away without even saying goodbye. She took your baby sister, but she left you behind. Your own mother didn't want you. You're afraid that she left to get away from you. So, you say mean things so that people won't think you care."

The sneer appeared to fall right off Lyda's face, replaced with fear. Her eyes darted about as if seeking an escape from a hungry bear chasing her down, intent on making her its main course. Royce saw the frightened, trapped expression. He did not stop.

"You think that something is wrong with you and that kids might not like you either. You pick on people you think are weak to get others to like you. But if you keep on being mean, you'll make it happen. They won't like you; nobody will. Some already don't; they're just afraid to make you mad." He ended it there.

Lyda now looked like she wished the hungry bear would eat her up, leaving nothing behind.

Another battle set up inside Royce. One part wanted to say sorry. The other part had fangs that wanted to sink in deeper. For some reason the fanged creature seemed like it had been there all along, caged but ready to pounce. A curious satisfaction flushed through him, even as he wondered if he had already blown it with his classmates and gape-mouthed teacher.

Later, at lunch, Royce noticed Lyda Hoskins eating alone, shrunk down in her chair. The earlier sensation came back. Lyda's feelings reached out to him. They came in the usual way, like a narrow wind that permeated his being, going straight to his heart. It filled him up. Most of the time, he got rid of the full feeling by speaking out. But that had gotten him horror eyes and shunning. Father said he needed to learn how to use it in wisdom. He should guard how and when he said things. Of course, it was too late to undo the earlier Lyda situation even if he cared to. He didn't care to. He really didn't.

The feeling remained though, in spite of his determined lack of caring, stinging his eyes as it sometimes did, causing water to gather. Royce could feel the moisture building.

"Is something wrong?" asked Chad.

Royce turned his head towards Chad who watched him with concern, a partially chewed meatball in his cheek to accommodate his speech. It took a moment for Royce to return fully to attend the question. Lyda's feelings persisted, urgent and intrusive. He saw Chad frown. That made him madder at Lyda. It wasn't his fault that Lyda had said mean things to him. She shouldn't have opened her mouth if she didn't want anything back. Now her emotions bombarded him trying to make him feel bad. And Chad had noticed.

Recalling the earlier constructed mental wall around Chrissy's pain that had worked a little bit, Royce tried something similar. With a great surge of will, he pushed back the feelings. In his mind, he built a stone wall to keep them from coming back. The push of water in his eyes ceased.

He looked over at Lyda and saw her hunch over suddenly like she'd been hit by an invisible blow. Royce didn't feel much except a soft thud against his new barricade. His success surprised him. He felt powerful.

"I'm fine, Chad. Better than fine."

And he thought it was true. When Chad started to cough as he often did, Royce was slow to respond, absently asking if he was alright. Royce's mind dwelt elsewhere. Now with a head free of others' feelings and emotions, there was room for other possibilities. Of course, one particular test would show the true strength of his new power.

When he got home, having chattered with Father the whole way, he said that he would go and see to Chrissy. He noted his father's pleased smile.

"Change your clothes first, son."

He did so and ran out to the barnyard. At first, he didn't recognize Chrissy. She appeared thinner and her movements were slow. Her eyes perked when she saw him with the carrots and apples. Royce put the food in the feeding trough along with fresh barley grass. He tentatively stroked her fur. He could sense the tap of her hope against his walled heart. It did not penetrate, however. Chrissy brayed pitifully at him, but he could no longer understand her. That part startled him. He had always understood her.

Another emotion grazed his defenses, but this time it had come from a distant part of him. It urged him to tear down his barrier and bury his face in Chrissy's coat and say sorry words. It almost happened. He made an opening, but shame entered, crowding out remorse. He slammed his wall back in place with firmer resolve. This time Chrissy's pleas were like the barely felt patter of a light rain.

"Good," he said out loud. "It works."

Chrissy continued to search his eyes with a naked, raw, want in her own eyes. Royce watched as the hope dwindled to almost gone. Finally, the donkey took a few listless bites of the food, before going to a dark corner to lie down. Royce stayed rooted where he was for reasons he couldn't answer. He stared at it for a long time before going back to the house to help Father with supper.

* * *

Royce was placing the forks and knives on the table when his mother came home from work. She looked at him, her face brimming with excitement and expectation. She kept her eyes on him for several beats before changing her expression to puzzlement.

Royce paused in setting the table. "You were right. School was much better with a friend. I'm glad I went back." He turned his lips up in a smile.

"I'm so glad, Royce," she said with sincere gladness in her voice. She crossed to where he was to envelope him in a hug and to kiss the top of his head.

When she let go, she lingered as if waiting for something. Royce went back to his chore with barely a brush of curiosity.

Later, when they were eating sweet peas and roasted chicken, Mother told of how her ad campaign had won an award.

Royce knew then why she had looked puzzled. Normally, her strong emotions came to him. Normally, he would have run to hug and congratulate her before she put her bag down. Normally. But he had changed. He was, well…normal. That was what he wanted. It was fine. He resented that Mother and Father kept locking eyes when they thought he wouldn't notice. He said, "That's great Mother."

He filled up the space where something else used to be with a lot of words. He was weary when he went to bed after taking only two bites of the first day of school coconut cake that Father had baked especially.

Normal felt funny.

He had a longing; something akin to hunger, except different. Something that food wouldn't fill up. His appetite was gone.

He did sleep, however. Chrissy was wailing again, but now it was just another night sound.

Chapter Four

Chrissy saw Royce nearly every day now, but it was a stranger in the skin of her once-friend. He was just a boy who fed her – or tried to feed her. He shrugged and walked away when she refused to eat. Chrissy tried to talk to him, but he didn't understand anymore. She became weaker and her coat dulled. She only took food when the father coaxed and crooned words. She knew the father was afraid she would go away to Forever if she didn't eat. So, she ate a little.

Most of the time, she didn't mind if she was going away forever, but a thread of 'perhaps' remained; so, she ate enough just in case. That hope leached her strength faster than not eating. Every time Royce was not the same with her, the pangs were like the sharp thorns of a briar bush, and the blow powerful, the way thunder sounded.

Still she hoped, remembering the way she and Royce used to frolic and play. She recalled wistfully, their prayers over food, their cuddles, and how they'd talked in their own special way, sharing secrets. And they had been happy.

Chrissy started getting angry at the memories that kept her yoked to hope. She hated hoping like she hated herself now. She wished that she could be like Dara: elegant, assured, and long-legged. But she was stuck with her body and her stupid hope.

The boomerang back and forth from misery to hope was nearly unbearable. Chrissy felt like one of those flies that tried to get back to the blue sky and sun but kept coming up against glass, only to repeat the futile effort; a macabre dance of stupidity. The fly never understood that nothing was going to change; it just kept hurling its body full force as if that time it could fly out. Finally, it struck itself gone forever. Chrissy was that fly.

Early one morning, long before the sun reached straight up, hope surprised her. Weighed down by the sorrow in her heart, her head nearly scraping the ground,

Chrissy returned to the barnyard after a listless sojourn to the meadow where she'd tortured herself with remembered joy. A sound disturbed her blanket of woe. She lifted her eyes. It was familiar but not. Her eyes stretched wide, startled by what they beheld.

"Howdy," brayed the newcomer.

Chrissy looked around in confusion. She noted the surroundings that were the usual barnyard sights. There was a ping of relief; for a minute there, she thought she had wandered into the land of Forever.

"What?" she asked weakly. She meant to ask something else, but her mind was dull from a lack of food and love.

"I said 'Howdy.'"

"You're a donkey," Chrissy said unnecessarily.

"I reckon I can't pull the sheep hair over your eyes." The other donkey let out a braying chuckle.

Chrissy could feel annoyance pushing through her depression. "What are you doing here?" Her voice came out stronger, her sentiments evident.

"Hold your britches. I'm just funning with you. My name is Sophia Christa. You can call me Sophy. I'm here for you."

"What do you mean?" Chrissy was more wary and wondered once again about the Forever place.

"I hear tell you need some comp'ny."

"Who told you that?"

"Well I can tell that you are mighty lonesome. You look sad-sack mournful the way your shoulders are draping the ground." Then Sophy said in a gentler tone, "I can tell your heart is full up with troubles. I'm here to help."

Chrissy started out to say that Sophia Christa should stick her nose in her own grass patch, but something in the other donkey's eyes and the soft sweet sympathy in her voice unraveled Chrissy's resolve. Instead, Chrissy dropped to the ground, as if her legs refused to carry her further. She gave a small, miserable bray. No strength was left to fight or pretend. Sophia dropped down too, laying her head on Chrissy's neck. Chrissy let her, giving a ragged sigh.

By and by, Sophy brought some barley grass and apple bits to Chrissy. She listened as the flow of troubles poured from the sad donkey. Sophy flapped her tail and blew into Chrissy's nose at all the right times. It was the way donkeys comforted each other. Soon, Chrissy was up and about, drinking water, getting stronger. She showed Sophy her important places and the good memories that went with them. A different Chrissy returned to the barnyard than had left that morning.

Even though her heart was still tender and sore, she felt unburdened, or rather, that someone was sharing the load. It was easier to walk and eat without the heavy weight. Still, when Royce came into the barn cloaked in the recently adopted careful nonchalance, to bring food, her body remembered its previous misery. Chrissy could feel the heft resettling on her body. But Sophia came alongside her, standing close enough to feel her coat. Step for step, she walked with Chrissy towards the boy whose presence bid hope to return.

Chrissy saw Royce blink a few times upon seeing the two of them, appearing to think the double donkeys was a problem with his eyes. His blinking apparently did not clear from his vision the new gray donkey accompanying the coffee colored Chrissy. He approached them with his head tilted in curiosity. He reached out to pat Chrissy in that new way of his, like he was bestowing a favor to a pitiful lesser being.

Sophy put her body between them. Royce was forced to back up. Chrissy saw his nostrils widen and heard the louder sound of his breath suck in. Sophy was firmly planted, making subtle moves to check Royce's frustrated motions towards Chrissy. It was a comical sight.

"She's my donkey!" Royce blurted out.

Sophy looked him in the eye and gave a very human-like snort. Chrissy, observing the funny spectacle had a smug sense of satisfaction when she saw Royce's eyes grow huge at the sound. He backed away once again.

Royce stomped to the feeding trough and dumped carrots, apples, and bananas from his knapsack, and put in fresh barley grass. He seemed mildly surprised by the addition of bananas; Chrissy preferred pears. He kept tossing his eyes over towards the two donkeys. When he finished, he headed with a stiff back to his house.

"See you later, Royce," Sophy said.

Chrissy didn't know whether to gape at Sophia or laugh at Royce's expression as he snatched his head around at the human words.

Royce darted his eyes around the yard looking for the speaker. Finally, his eyes rested on first Chrissy, then Sophy, narrowed and suspicious. They just tried to look as donkey-like as possible, which was easy since they were indeed donkeys.

At last, with a showy shrug and wrinkled brow, Royce left. When he was out of sight, Chrissy pounced on Sophy.

"What...how...?"

* * *

Royce was spooked. It was one thing to imagine that he understood Chrissy; it was another thing to think he heard actual human words from a donkey. He tried to tell himself that he didn't hear what he heard. It didn't work. Maybe it was a trick, or maybe his mind was really cracked.

He wanted to ask his father, but he didn't want to sound crazy. He did, however, ask at dinner about the extra donkey.

"Father," Royce said, "that grey donkey, uh... how come we have another one?"

"Chrissy is lonely, so Sophy is here to keep her company," Father said. He went back to eating blueberry cobbler.

"She's kinda strange," Royce said as he stabbed at blueberries.

"Oh?" asked Father.

"Uh, well, she, uh...isn't so friendly like Chrissy," Royce answered.

"Chrissy likes her. She's eating again and she's not crying anymore." Father took another bite of cobbler, darting Mother a look that Royce had come to hate. "Chrissy has a friend now."

At his words, Royce felt a thousand darts in his heart, somehow penetrating the barrier around it. He hurriedly tried to block the impact, but he was only partially successful. The half-eaten cobbler on his plate no longer looked appealing. He pushed it away.

That night he had a hard time sleeping and not because of Chrissy's constant crying. That surely was not it. He heard neither sniffle nor sigh from Chrissy.

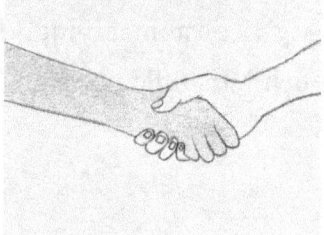

Chapter Five

A few weeks later, just when the leaf colors peaked in fullest glory, Chad and Royce sat in the back seat of Chad's mom's car. She had picked them up from school like she'd done a lot lately. Instead of her usual deliberately cheerful chatter, she was quiet. She had an anxious and weary look on her face. Royce could also see fear in her eyes.

Chad was the opposite and had been so all day. He'd been very talkative and using words like pal and buddy an extra amount of times. Even now he sat close, shoulder touching shoulder. When Royce repositioned, putting space between them, Chad had reattached as if there were a magnetic homing device in his arm. Consequently, both boys ended up huddled on the passenger side of the car. Royce knew something was coming, but was reluctant to open to it, thus he'd hidden behind his barrier. It was just for a little while he told himself. But it had been most of the day. Now Chad's mother forced him to face things.

"Chad is going away for a bit," she said in a voice with breaks in it.

With a sigh, Royce let in enough emotions to respond in a proper way. He turned his body towards Chad, which was awkward given their up-close proximity. He placed his hand on his friend's shoulder to show him comfort. He knew that Chad would not want words. He gave a few anyway.

"I think you are very brave, friend."

Chad scowled but gave a nod.

"I'll text you often," Royce promised. "I'll see you when you get back. We'll play Rummikub." He saw the doubting hope in Chad's eyes.

"Thank you," Chad said with grave sincerely.

When they arrived at Royce's house, Chad got out too. He held out his hand. Royce took it and they shook hands in solemn imitation of their fathers. Chad held on, giving a desperate squeeze. Royce returned the pressure with his own desperation to make a promise that was not in his power to keep.

At last Chad released his grip and got back in the car. Royce noticed the sparkle of Chad's mother's tears. He watched and waved until the car had disappeared from sight.

He was sad. It would be long days without Chad. At the same time, he felt a little lighter. He thought about it and realized that Chad's ever-present fears had weighed a lot. What must it be like for Chad to carry it? Royce vowed to be a better friend and keep in touch while he was gone.

In the meantime, he had nothing to do. It was Friday and he wouldn't have school again until the following Wednesday. Inside the house, he placed his jacket on a hook and searched out his father. He found him in the kitchen putting a roast in the oven while talking to someone on the phone. Father pointed his head towards the fruit and vegetables for the donkeys, indicating that Royce should do the feeding.

Royce put his jacket back on and took slow steps to the barn. He'd managed to avoid feeding them since the last disturbing visit weeks before. He was relieved to see neither Sophy nor Chrissy. Sort of. Curiosity had other ideas. He didn't entirely want to, but after depositing their food in the trough, he went searching for the two donkeys.

He headed for the meadow first. Usually he enjoyed the changing look of the vegetation. The foliage was sparser, but the colors of the leaves more than made up for that. The crispy feel in the air and the crunch under his feet was a faraway joy now. Like something in a picture album that you looked at with fond wistfulness. As he approached, memories poked at him of peace and companionship. He felt confused and attacked by the longing that glommed on to him. He tried to block it out and shake it off, but it clung. He tried thinking about Chad, but that was heavy too. He stopped. He didn't have to put up with the assault. The trees and bushes had betrayed him, not offering the peace and contentment he was used to. He turned around to go back home; the donkeys were probably safe and cozy together.

Royce took several steps towards home, but his feet stopped again at the sound of voices. He cocked his head. Yes, those were voices alright. Who was in the meadow? Once more he changed direction, approaching slowly. He was more curious than fearful. As he got closer the words were more distinct.

"I wish I had longer legs," he heard.

"Well, you ain't got them, so quit wasting your

wishes."

Royce crept closer to see who was talking about wishes. When he reached the clearing, he was puzzled. He searched the area, but he only saw Sophy and Chrissy settled on the ground, looking in his direction. An incredulous suspicion began rising in him, but before it could take shape, he received confirmation.

"Howdy, Royce," Sophy said, looking in his direction. Royce felt his mouth open, and his jaw drop and stick there.

"Well, don't just dawdle there all bug-eyed and gap-jawed. Git on over here. We were waiting on you."

Royce's legs obeyed while his mind tried to make sense. He looked at Chrissy.

"Can you talk, too?"

"I've always talked," Chrissy said in a short tone.

"But not in human words."

"You used to understand me."

Royce was uncomfortable and shifted from foot to foot.

"Cut out that dancing and sit on down for a spell," Sophy directed.

Again, Royce obeyed. He couldn't say why. It was like he was supposed to. He sat near Chrissy and out of habit reached to caress her, but she stiffened and moved away. Royce was hurt. He looked at her with baleful eyes, but she didn't look back.

"I reckon when a wasp stings you, you ain't hankering to stick your hand back in the nest," Sophy said.

"I'm not a wasp!" Royce said. "And she used to be nice."

"You used to be nice," Sophy said matter-of-factly.

"I don't like you," Royce said.

"You don't like my true words."

"What do you know? You're just a dumb animal." Royce was getting heated.

"The truth is always the truth, even if it comes from the mouth of a donkey," Sophy said calmly.

Royce jumped up with his fists in a ball. "Why am I talking to you anyway; you're not my boss. You're just a stupid donkey. You're tricking me, trying to make me look like a fool. I'm telling Father."

Sophy and Chrissy gave him steady looks. He didn't hear laughter, but he could feel it. And something else. He ran from there, but the compassion and understanding mixed up with their mirth followed him all the way home. He did not mention to his father that he had a conversation in human language with two donkeys. Neither did he tell Chad when he texted him after supper.

* * *

Chrissy was a little mad at Sophy too. Just a little. She admitted to herself that she had enjoyed how uncomfortable Royce had been. And she also acknowledged that Royce's attempts to touch her were both unwelcome and welcome. She was thrilled to be back with him in their special place, but she was scared to trust him. She felt bad that he had fled, though. She blamed Sophy.

"You didn't have to be so mean," she said after Royce had run off.

"You could have asked him to stay," said Sophy.

After moments of saying nothing, Chrissy asked, "Do you think he will come back?"

"Not tonight, young lady. But don't worry your noggin. Like I explained before; our mouths were opened for a purpose, and it has to do with your boy, Royce."

"I don't understand all this," Chrissy said.

"By and by, you will. Now let's go get some vittles. Starting tomorrow we'll need our strength something extra. I sure hope they didn't skimp on the bananas."

Chapter Six

The next morning, after a restless night, Royce rose early, got his own breakfast, grabbed a jacket and headed to the meadow. Maybe he had been dreaming or maybe the voices were a different way of hearing with his gift. Sitting among the maybes, surprising him, was a hope that it had been real. That excited and perplexed him.

Reaching the meadow, breathless in his hurry, Royce saw the donkeys in nearly the same place as the evening before. He slowed, approached them timidly, waiting for them to say the first words. No one said a thing. Chrissy still barely looked at him, her glance sliding away just before reaching his eyes. Sophy had no issue with contacting Royce's eyes. He saw kindness there, but also challenge.

"So, can you really talk or not?" Royce finally blurted.

"I believe your ears told you the answer to that," was all Sophy said.

"But it's not usual," Royce said defensively. "How am I supposed to tell what's real?"

"Well, who are you talking to right now, young fella?" Sophy smirked and Royce could feel his face heat up. He noticed that Chrissy lifted her head, giving Sophy one of those looks that went on between Father and Mother. He was irritated and gratified in equal parts.

With a sigh, Sophy said, "Yes, it's real, and I know it's weird. But before ya freak out, you should know that it's not the first time that one of my kind has up and started talking to you humans in y'all's own language. But more 'bout that later. Why don't you sit on down and I'll explain some things to you about donkeys and how special we are," she cast a sidelong glance at Chrissy, "even if our legs aren't as long as a horse's."

Royce sat down leaning against an oak tree. He was in touching distance of Chrissy and his hand twitched, wanting to bury itself in her coat, but he caught himself right before making contact. He turned towards Sophy and waited for her to begin. He was eager to hear what she had to say.

"First off, my full name is Sophia Crista. Like Chrissy and me, most all donkeys have a form of the name Christopher or Christophera. All of us donks wear that name proudly. It means Bearer of Christ. Our high-falutin' name is Equus Africanus Asinus."

"Wow that's new to me," said Chrissy. "It's an important sounding name."

"There's a lot more you'll be learning about our kind. Most people don't know our real name and we have been called other names that are downright mean."

"But all of you don't talk," Royce said.

"True. Only for special occasions." said Sophy.

Royce opened his mouth to say something else, but Sophy beat him to it.

"I reckon you're wondering why I'm breaking the language barrier. I'll tell you straight out, I'm not sure why our mouths were opened for human-speak, or why one of my kind was picked to carry The Blessed Son. The Sacred Book says that World-Maker uses the foolish things of the world to put the wise-in-their-own-eyes to shame. I'm a foolish thing. Leastwise, that's my reputation. And I'm happy to serve World-Maker's purposes."

"But why were you chosen in particular?" asked Royce. "Are you more 'foolish' than other donkeys?" He made air quotes when he said the word foolish.

"I don't rightly know. I ponder to myself: Who am I to deserve such an honor? My donkey kin used to tease me something fierce, saying that I was strange because my best friend was a boy. It was powerful lonesome sometimes."

Royce gave her a sharp look. He heard the leftover pain in Sophy's voice. He knew what that was like. Something got softer around his heart. He nodded at Sophy in understanding.

"Maybe some things will be cleared when I explain how we donkeys went from being labeled an ass, to our new name of Christ-bearer." Sophy said to Royce, "You can bet that your story is all tangled up with ours. That's how World-Maker works. He's not a one-trick pony, that's for sure. So, lean in and hike up them ears…"

Chapter Seven

S ophy recited a story from the scriptures:

World-Maker opened up the mouth of the donkey and gave him human speech. And the donkey said to Balaam: 'You have beat me three times now. What did I do to deserve that?' Balaam said, "Because you've been messing around with me making me look like a fool! If I had a sword, I would have killed you by now.' The donkey replied to Balaam, "I'm your trusty donkey on whom you've ridden for years. Have I ever done anything to harm you?'

Balaam said, 'No you haven't.'
Then World-Maker opened Balaam eyes to
see what was going on: He saw World-Maker's
angel blocking the road, brandishing a sword.
Balaam fell to the ground, putting his face in the
dirt.
World-Maker angel said to him: 'Why have you
beaten your poor donkey these three times? I
have come here to block your way because you
are going the wrong way, doing things wrong.
The donkey saw me and turned away from me
three times. She saved you. If she hadn't, I
would have killed you by now, but not the don-
key. I would have spared her.'

Royce had heard the story before, and even though it was in the Sacred Book, a part of him hadn't believed it. He saw things differently now. "So, it was true," he said in wonder. "Wow," said Chrissy. "That donkey was so brave."

Royce saw that her head was lifted in a proud way; not like the low to the ground way she had been carrying it lately. He felt a pang. He wanted to block it, but he let it remain. He'd had a big part in that. His own head shifted low.

"Before we get on to my ancestor talking to Balaam, you should know that it is the male Donkeys that are called Asses or Jacks. A female is a Jenny. Every last one of us donkeys, male and female alike, get thrown in the same barn and suffer being labeled lazy, stupid, and stubborn. Some still think of us that a' way. Even a long time after the Balaam incident, we have remained the butt of your jokes. It's like when teachers forced school children to wear donkey ears for punishment when they didn't know the right answers. That kinda hurts my pride, but I've got a thick hide.

"It seems to me that it's the humans that are stupid," said Chrissy. "I already know that they can be mean." She didn't look at Royce, but her words met the new soft spot around his heart.

Sophy continued, "Seeing as how we were never thought of in a good light, I reckon y'all can understand why Balaam was knocked out of his britches, bless his heart, when my ancestor started speaking mankind words. That prophet did not expect his beast of burden to up and become a messenger of God. My blessed ancestor had to bear up under a beating just for trying to save his master's hiney.

"I get it. Y'all humans have a hard enough time hearing God through y'all's own truth tellers or prophets, especially if it doesn't match up with the picture in y'all's head. So, I don't take offense – well, I do a little. But this ain't totally about that. Call to mind Balaam's near miss and perk up your noggin as I go over some of y'all's history with God-Speakers."

Sophy pushed out her front legs and arched her back up in a stretch before settling back down in the grass. Royce pulled his knees up to his chest and wrapped his arms around them, bracing himself for what might come next.

"Speaking of weird…" Sophy said. "The Mighty One's messages have come from unlikely, even creepy, sources. There was that burning bush that didn't quite burn. And what about that hand not attached to a body, somehow writing on a wall. Now that sho' nuff is horror movie stuff. Wouldn't ya like to have been a fly on that wall to see folks' reactions?

Royce stretched his eyes wide and shook his head in a firm 'no.' A hand writing on its own was not on his wish list. Sophy chuckled at his expression.

"Then scariest thing of all, especially to some menfolk," Sophy paused dramatically, then said sarcastically, "was when the messages came from a woman. That's all I'm going to say about that, 'ceptin' sometimes donkeys get more respect than women folk." She gave a few tsks before continuing. "Of course, some messengers had tails and long ears. Ahem, ahem." Sophy lifted her nose in mock haughtiness, swished her tail and wiggled her ears.

Chrissy and Royce laughed and looked at each other in shared glee, before Chrissy suddenly looked away.

Sophy leaned in and spoke in a barely audible tone, "And they've come from a whisper in the wind with nary a person anywheres. And if you think that was strange, bless my helping hooves, the messengers have come in some pretty strange packages too. There was that camel hair wearer. I hear tell those locusts he chowed on were lip-smacking good with honey. Y'all should try 'em." She grinned at Royce's grimace.

"Remember that there one that thought he could duck out on the All-Seeing, and found himself holed up in the belly of a big ole fish? Uh… ewwwww."

"Jonah!" Royce shouted out like he was on a game show competing for a prize.

"Yup, on the snout. And from the Tear Fountain Hall of Fame we have The Weeper. I reckon he cared so much, the caring just poured right out of his eyes. Just so you know, we donks can't protect ourselves from moisture, so pu-leeze stay away when you feel tears cropping up." She paused to nod her head with emphasis.

"Now here's one of my favorites. There was a Warrior Woman that was braver than all the menfolk clumped together. She did what they were afraid to do." Sophy jumped up and pointed her ears forward, back and forward again. She repeated the action three times. "Donkey salute!" she explained.

Chrissy pointed her ears in imitation of Sophy. Royce raised his hand to his forehead and away like he'd seen military people do. "People salute," he said with a grin.

They all took a moment to be pleased with themselves. Then Sophy lowered to the ground again and continued.

"And let's not forget that long-haired muscle man."

"Samson!" Royce cried out, smiling wide, pleased that he knew who Sophy was talking about. "He was super strong."

"Right again, young fella. Did y'all know that a donkey is stronger than a horse?"

"Really?" asked Chrissy, a bemused look on her face that turned smug. Royce guessed that she might have been thinking of Dara.

"Yes siree! And here's something else to chaw on. Chrissy, did you know that even our body parts were involved in World-Maker's great work? That same strong feller, Samson, slew a thousand men with the jawbone of one of my kind. I reckon ya never know what After-Life will bring. You think you're done with this life, then, whammo, your bones get a work-out." Sophy chuckled.

She changed her tone to reverence. "And, of course, there was The Blessed One who we all know was so much more than a mere carpenter. He wasn't what folks were expecting. Yup, a lot of those folks were not exactly your everyday normal people. Not many of them lived high on the hog, either."

Sophy stood up. "This is from the Sacred Book:

'What did you go out in the desert to see? A reed swaying in the wind? If not, what did you think you were going to see? Some man dressed up in expensive clothes? No, those who wear fine clothes live in royal palaces. So what did you go out to see? A prophet? Yes, you did, and it was more than a prophet.'

"I didn't make that up. Those there are the words from Jesus, Joseph's boy; the Blessed One that our kind had the privilege of carrying around during important times. He certainly had a right smart way of saying things.

"I heard he said those words to his followers in Galilee after he got the news that his cousin, John, the Prophet and locust-eater, had been shoved in a dank prison for truth-telling."

"That wasn't fair," said Royce, "He was just trying to help people."

"Just like Balaam's donkey," said Chrissy. "Balaam hurt the donkey when the donkey was only trying to protect him." Royce heard the pain in Chrissy's voice and felt like she was talking about more than the story. The pang in his heart went deeper.

"Here's the rub," Sophy was saying, "most times we donkeys are considered a poor man's animal. And thinking on it, that's not too far off from how some of y'all's prophets were looked at. Neither man nor beast get much respect in those situations."

"A whole lot of y'all's truth tellers came from humble beginnings. Some came from poor families. They came from enslaved people who worked like donkeys. There was that woman who was treated like she was worth nothing 'cause she couldn't have any babies. And we can't leave out the fisher folks, toiling on the water from sunup to sundown, sometimes their nets coming up empty. And now we come again to The Blessed One that came from Nazareth. They said that nothing good could come from that backwoods village. But y'all know that turned out to be horse doodie."

Royce snickered, and so did Chrissy. This time she did not stop herself. Royce felt his heart spark up in hope.

Looking pleased, Sophy continued. "Y'all's prophets got asked to do some mighty interesting things. The whole lot of them were like some kind of superheroes. They stopped the sun, made it rain, and brought down big ole temples. Can you imagine making a divide in the middle of the ocean? And earlier on, one of them dudes built a ship big enough to hold near 'bout the whole world.

"Wow," marveled Royce, "the whole world fit on a ship?"

"Well, it could have; but some didn't make the trip."

Royce frowned as he let that sink in.

"Yuppers, some of those things just make me sit on my haunches and say, Good gracious alive! Those are some downright real attention getters. Now, admit it, hearing a donkey talking certainly grabs your attention. And it sho' nuff saved Balaam's . . .uh, bootie."

Royce raised his hand like he was in school. At Sophy's nod he asked, "How come God wanted to get their attention. And how come you and Chrissy are talking now? Whose attention is He trying to get now?" Royce was afraid it was about him.

Chrissy spoke up too. "It can't be because... you know...that thing with me and, you know, what happened. Our stuff seems so little compared to other things. We can't be that important?"

"The whole passel of us is important to World-Maker. He might focus on one person for a minute, but it is always bigger than that. And you two were special way before now. Not every human and donkey can understand each other. And Chrissy, you can use human words now, but I betcha didn't know that besides me, no other donkey can understand human language like you can. You are what some like to call weird."

Chrissy's jaw was stretched wide for several beats. "You mean I'm special?" There was wonder in her voice.

"Even without long legs," Sophy said.

"I'm not like everybody else either," said Royce. "Why are we like this? What are we supposed to do? Being 'special,'" he did air quotes, "hasn't worked out well for me."

"That remains to be seen," said Sophy. "But I do know that World-Maker snags your attention for a good purpose. Y'all call us donks stubborn, but you humans can give us a right good run for that title. Most-Faithful shines up to you even when you are acting like a butt."

"But why would he be nice to me – to us if we do bad things?" Royce asked.

"Why? I reckon it's what you call love. I'm thinking that means that Abba loves you enough to pull out every tool that it takes for you to not grow up womp-sided. He wants you to stop being so stubborn so he can teach you Truth, to protect you and get you ready for what He has planned. He wants you to know the good news that you can change for the better. In His mercy, He wants to heal y'all's minds and help you to get shed of bad things that chain you down. Then you can be free to live full-up lives and have a heap of joy."

"If that's true; that's really nice of Him?" Royce said, hoping it was.

"It's for sure true."

Like Jesus, who was also a Carpenter, said when he was chewing the cud in the Temple at Mount of Olives, *'The truth will set you free.'* And he also said, *'I'll send my messenger on a head of you, he'll prepare the road before you have to go.'* Jesus, who was a Prophet, was referring to his cousin, John who was also a Messenger."

Sophy leaned back on her hind legs in another

stretch. She got up and stamped the ground a few times. "Whelp, I see by the sun that it's time for chawing on something besides words." She aimed a meaningful look in Royce's direction.

"I'll go and get our lunch," Royce said, not missing the hint. He looked at the ground and back up at Sophy, and in a shy voice said, "Thank you for talking to me. If you're not too tired, maybe you can explain things some more -- after we eat, of course."

"I'm inclined to do just that. That's why I showed up in the first place. So, scurry on back. And don't be forgetting the bananas."

Royce looked over at Chrissy and wanted to say something but couldn't find the words. Maybe hope was feeding his imagination, but he thought she gave him a small nod, so, he turned and hurried to his house.

***

Royce ran into the kitchen, grabbed the knapsack and whipped Chrissy's favorite fruit and veggies inside of it. He was heading back out the door to get barley grass when his mother laid a hand on his arm.

"Hold on for a minute; aren't you going to eat lunch?"

Royce stopped in his tracks, realizing that he had not said anything to his mother and father who were both in the kitchen. "Oh, hi, Mother, Father. I'm bringing food to the donkeys." He started to leave again, but this time his father stopped him.

"Let me make you a ham sandwich," he said.

Royce was becoming impatient. "The donkeys don't eat sandwiches."

"But you do. Sit down while I make it."

It was that tone that Royce recognized; pleasant on the outside but firm on the inside. He sat, wiggling his foot.

So," said Father, "what are you and the donks up to today?"

"We're just talking."

"Talking?"

"I mean, hanging out, doing stuff." Royce avoided his father's eyes.

"Even with weird Sophy?"

Royce peered at his father with suspicion. He thought he detected a laugh in his voice. Father was calmly securing thick slabs of ham between Mother's homemade bread. A glance at his mother showed she had a smiling expression as she sipped her favorite Earl Grey tea.

"Well, she is weird, but I don't mind it so much anymore," said Royce. He caught his father's eye and said, "Weird isn't always bad."

Father handed him two wrapped sandwiches and some bananas. "True. Weird isn't always bad."

As he was putting the sandwiches in his sack, Royce noticed the now-common exchange of looks between his parents. He rolled his eyes – but not too much-- and rushed to the barn with a small smile on his face.

Chapter Eight

Chrissy heard Sophy chuckle. She perked her ears but did not move her gaze away from the path where Royce would hopefully soon reappear.

"He'll be along directly. Your staring won't bring him back any faster."

Chrissy nearly protested, but instead asked sheepishly, "Do you think he'll come back?" She took her eyes off the path to look at Sophy.

"As sure as blackbirds have wings."

"I think he's sorry for being mean to me. Do you think he's sorry?" Before Sophy could answer, Chrissy swiveled her head back towards the wooded path, having heard hurried footfalls moving in their direction.

Soon Royce appeared with his knapsack hanging from his shoulders, the rise and fall of his chest faster than usual. Chrissy could hear the pumped up beat of his heart. He stopped, letting the pack plunk to the ground.

Now that he was back, Chrissy was relieved, but didn't know what to do. She just pawed the ground in a fidgety way.

"Where's Sophy?" Royce asked.

Chrissy looked behind her and all around, but the older donk was nowhere in sight. "I don't know, but I'm sure she'll be back."

"Chrissy." Royce looked at her with a contrite expression.

"I know," said Chrissy hastily. "It's fine."

"No, it's not fine. If it was me, I mean if someone treated me that way, it would make me sad, and I guess mad, too. I'm sorry, Chrissy, that I was mean to you. I don't know all the reasons why… you've always been a good friend and you didn't do anything to make me hurt you. I got twisted up. The way I treated you…I don't deserve…I hope you can forgive me. I'll try to be a friend to you again, if you still want me to." Royce looked anxious and hopeful.

Chrissy's heart melted at his pleading tones and

big sorrowful eyes. The pain around her heart let up, but soreness remained. She could tell that it would be that way for a while. Still she said, "I forgive you, Royce. I want to be your friend again, but now there is a shadow where there used to be only light. I feel skittish."

"I understand," Royce said.

Chrissy was relieved and a little sad, "I know things will never go back, but maybe we can be a new thing. Maybe it will be better. In time."

"In time," agreed Royce.

"You're a sight for my rumbling belly," Sophy said suddenly reappearing, causing Royce and Chrissy to jump. "Let's see what you're packing."

Royce spread out the food. Sophy gave a pleased bray at the sight of the bananas. Royce was glad Father added them. And without saying anything, the three, in accord, lifted their faces upward in thanksgiving.

They ate with few words between them. After they'd had enough, Royce sat again with his back against the oak tree. Chrissy settled near him; not touching, but in reachable distance.

"I'm right proud that y'all made up," Sophy said.

"How did you know?" asked Royce, a little embarrassed. "Were you spying on us?"

"Not directly. I didn't have to. I was quite a stretch

away, but I heard y'all just fine. We donkeys have some awful good hearing. In the desert, we can hear one of our own kind from sixty miles away. We wiggle our ears 'round so the sound comes in clear. We don't wanna miss a thing. It's in our best interest, so we can know what's coming. You can never tell what might try to sneak up on ya. Maybe y'all humans should try opening up y'all's ears better."

Royce chuckled, "I don't think I'll be able to hear from sixty miles away, no matter how much I wiggle my ears."

"That's rightly so," said Sophy, "but I'm talking about a different kind of hearing. You know, and I know, that humans don't always wanna hear what your prophets have to say. When it hits too close, your kind is liable to stick your fingers in your ears and slam them eyes shut tight. Y'all pop up with all manner of excuses of why you shouldn't have to listen. That prophet is too drunk. That one doesn't drink enough. I know his family; who is he to tell me what's what? And on and on."

"Well, you can guess who had some two cents about that. Jesus. He was big brother to James, Joseph, Simon, Judas and a slew of sisters.

"Your ears are open, but you don't seem to hear a thing. Your eyes are open, but you don't

see a thing…. People are ornery! They stick their fingers in their ears, so they won't have to listen; they squeeze their eyes tight so that they won't have to look. If they dealt with me head on I could heal them. But they won't let me."

"Oh," said Chrissy, "I think I get it. That's why World-Maker has to do things to make people look."

"Yup. People folks should be more like animals and be able to tell apart the true from the fake. The Blessed One said that his sheep recognized his voice."

"It's important to tell the True voice from the False voice. We donks are sensitive and protective about our ears. It would be wrong-headed for you to try to touch them. We have to trust you first. If you try to pull our ears, you might get a kick in you hind parts.

"I'm thinking that y'all need to be more protective of y'all's ears. It boggles me how y'all don't think nothing 'bout letting in false voices. I tell you what," Sophy said looking at Royce, "if you get honest with yourself and recognize the bear snares of 'why,' you might not fall into a trap."

"I think that maybe I got caught in a trap, Sophy," said Royce sincerely. "But I'm confused about all the ways how."

"I can start you out with some things to be on the lookout for. Sometimes you plum don't know the true voice when you hear it? Reading the Sacred Book can help with that. There are also times when those fake messengers scratch your ears just right and say what you're itching to hear."

Royce nodded slowly, as if recognizing some true things in what Sophy said.

"Maybe you can't bear to see yourselves in a bad light," Sophy said. "Could be that having to change makes you want to kick and whinny. 'Cause doing things different can be downright uncomfortable. Most of all, watch out for the deceiving voices. Those voices can promise you things that seem like freedom, but are really a slave pit. Remember the thirty pieces of silver," Sophy nodded solemnly.

Chrissy did remember. She knew how the God-Son's friend had betrayed him for those pieces of metal that meant so much to Royce's people. It made humans weak. She wondered if Chad's family had this metal.

"Y'all may not like me saying this," Sophy continued, "but I think that your noses get stuffed so full of lies that the truth smells like death. And your ears so plugged that this may all sound like hee-haw to you." Again, Sophy gave Royce a piercing look, making him squirm.

"Sometimes you can put up a barricade, and a voice that once was clear to you now sounds like a donkey braying."

Chrissy could tell that Sophy's words hit close to Royce's heart; his head went low. She wanted to comfort him, but memories of his foot pushing her away, blocked her from doing anything. She sighed to herself instead.

"That plumb makes me wanna up and quit sometimes," Sophy was saying. "It feels like everything I say runs up on dead or insensitive ears. But I'll keep up the racket even when the very ones you are trying to help, up and turn on you."

Sophy kept her eyes on Royce. "It's hard to bear up under the truth. For some, when the truth comes up against their lie-packed ears, they hurt the ones trying to help them. Y'all have chucked stones at them, turned them into lion food, and tossed them into prison. Y'all sawed your own kind in two; you whipped them, kicked them, and called them bad names. You turn their truth into jokes -- anything so as not to hear. And The Precious One, y'all nailed to wood."

Chrissy saw the compassion in Sophy's eyes as she steadily watched her words reach Royce in his sensitive place. In soft, loving tones she said, "Blessed is the person who allows himself to be washed in the truth. To deny the truth is like a fella beating up his own donkey."

Sophy paused for a bit. "Here are some wise words spoken by Jesus the Teacher:

> 'Watch out for fake prophets. They come to you wearing sheep's clothing, but on the inside they are wild savage wolves. You'll recognize good trees from bad trees by the kind of fruit they grow. Do grapes come from bushes with thorns?' And he also said, 'sheep follow their own shepherd because they are familiar with his voice. They don't dare follow a stranger's voice, instead, they will scatter because they don't recognize it.'"

Silence stretched out among them, speaking in ways that words couldn't. Chrissy felt like the message was a living, active presence among them. She could see various expressions chasing across Royce's face, and how his shoulders had stiffened as if bracing against sharp, northern winds. She found that she held her breath, waiting to see if the words had penetrated her boy's skin and fenced places. She also wanted badly to nuzzle his cheek with hers, to let him have the comfort of her fur running through his fingers. But she didn't move.

She saw when his shoulders softened, his expression cleared, and his fists loosen; like a tree letting go of the dead leaves it had once gripped tightly.

"Sometimes," Royce said into the heavy quiet, "the false voice is from your own head."

"Yup," Sophy agreed.

"What do I do? Is there hope for me?" Royce asked.

"Of course, there is hope. I can tell that you are listening and letting words wrap around and inside of you. You are gonna be alright. Just don't stop now."

Royce's eyes glistened with water that didn't pour down his cheeks. Chrissy hoped that her boy would keep on listening, letting healing words inside of him. What if he changed back into the fenced in Royce when Chad came around? She was suddenly aware that she could feel a bit of his emotions. It wasn't like it had been before when she knew his feelings. She wondered if that was partly because they could talk to each other with human words now.

Like you Royce," Sophy was saying, "Merciful Heaven and O Happy Day, sometimes folks propped their ears open and heard the Messengers. They were healed from all manner of things like leprosy, broken minds, bleeding problems, you name it. They turned a li'l bit of food to a whole heap. Ornery, hard-headed people changed, and kept on changing. Those that used to murder people became the most loving folks ever. Whole towns avoided the wrecking ball. Peace settled in hearts as they became free from all their chains. Mercy became the first name of those that used to be hateful. To see it makes you want to do a jig of joy."

"But those Messengers had to go through a lot of bad things, and some people will never listen." Royce scrunched his forehead.

"That's right. Telling the truth don't set well with a lot of folks. But it's worth it if even just a few are snatched from the slavery of lies. Truth-tellers have to accept that Glad and Sad are bundled up together on their backs. You have to have deep caring to carry it. Not everyone is built for it. But it has to start in your own barnyard."

Chapter Nine

After Royce had fed Sophy and Chrissy, and was sharing a meal with his father and mother, the two donks, in quiet communion, watched the sky deepen its blue enough to reveal the points of light sparkling above them. The beauty was the kind that Chrissy never got tired of looking at. She was glad that she could take notice again. Her sadness had been a mist that blocked out the glory of World-Maker's best creations.

Chrissy thought about the many things she had heard about her kind and Royce's. Her heart was topped up with gratitude for Sophy.

"Sophy, if it wasn't for you, Royce might never

have come back. Thank you for caring."

"You are surely welcome, Chrissy. Everyone gets tangled up in the weeds once in a while."

"It seemed like they were going to cover him whole," Chrissy said.

"Like I said, I'm right proud of that young fella for owning up to his wrongs. How are you feeling about things?"

"Well, I'm glad he saw how badly he treated me. We'll see how things go."

"Do you mean you don't believe him?"

"Oh, I believe he's telling the truth. But it's his turn to see how it feels."

"Well, that don't exactly smack of grace. You can do better."

Chrissy huffed, raising her tone, "How come I have to carry his grass? He hurt me bad."

"Aw, that's the long and tall of it; he hurt you, and you want to hurt him back."

"That would be fair." The huff left her voice, "But I think I'm scared. Now that I know what heart hurt is like, I'm skittish that it will happen again. I'm afraid that if I let him back in my fence, he'll disappoint me, and I can't take it."

"I reckon he will disappoint you again. That's the

way of it. The ones you want the most from, can't always deliver. It's a right impossible job. We have to decide if the rest of what they are is enough for us. Nobody says you have to be friends. You might choose to chuck it all away. But none of that half-way horse patootie. That ain't fair to Royce."

Chrissy became indignant, "Fair! Was he fair to me? You know how his treatment tore my heart to ant-sized shreds. I suffered. Don't you care anymore about me?" Chrissy put hurt in her bray.

"You know better than to ask if I care. Are you trying to hurt me, too? How much does Royce have to suffer before you decide to forgive him?" Sophy moved closer to Chrissy and nuzzled her neck and blew into her nose. Speaking softly, she said, "You know my sorrow ran deep for you. And I know that your heart sore will take a while to heal. But it won't heal proper if you let in bitter water. Royce owned up to his mistake; that takes a lot of courage. It also takes courage to open your fence back up. Think on those things."

* * *

Royce texted with Chadwick for a long while until the other boy's mother suggested that it was time for her son to go to sleep. After, he sat in his room pondering the things that Sophy had mentioned, wondering how he was going to fit in both Chrissy and Chadwick. He hadn't mentioned anything about his talking donkeys to Chad. He knew it was not the time to bring it up. Maybe things would be different when his friend returned – if his friend returned. Some things he didn't 'know' in his special way. What was the use of it if it didn't show up when he needed it? He let out a heavy sigh, at the end of which there was a rap on his door. Mother popped her head in.

"I've made popcorn with extra butter, and we can watch Princess Bride," Mother offered. It was one of Royce's favorites.

Royce nestled between his parents on the couch munching on popcorn and his dad's homemade chocolate-covered raisins. It was good to laugh. He laughed hard in all the usual places. He also cried in unexpected places. When he couldn't stop, Father paused the movie and Mother gathered him in her lap, though his legs dangled almost to the floor. She murmured, stroked his hair, punctuating it with kisses. Father wrapped them both in his strong arms, laying his head on Royce's. It was what they called a Royce sandwich. It had been a long time since they had been that way because Royce had decreed that he was too big. He didn't feel too big now. Other things seemed too big.

"Royce," Father said, after Royce's tears had become weary little hiccups, "You don't have to carry heavy things alone. We are right here. We've got you."

* * *

The following morning, Royce didn't go to the pre-teen class at church; he chose to sit between his parents. He was grateful that even though he was feeling a million years old and dealing with big things, he was still their little boy. He needed their strength.

Watching their reverent worship, he realized something. They could be strong because they weren't carrying heavy things by themselves either. The true Mighty One had 'got' them. Royce felt safer. That made him think of Chrissy and Sophy. Sophy had Chrissy's back because he, Royce, had left it uncovered. Instead of hanging his head low again, he lifted it up and prayed that he would not leave her uncovered again. Even if she never trusted him again.

When he got home, he exchanged his church clothes for meadow wear. He selected the choicest edibles for the two donks; he remembered the bananas for Sophy. They were not in the barn, so he walked to the meadow, finding them there. After the meal, Chrissy settled right up against Royce. He slowly put out his hand to stroke her coat. She let him. A lump formed in Royce's throat. At first, it was stiff and awkward; but eventually, as Sophy resumed her storytelling, they forgot to be self-conscious, heeding the tale that was bigger than them, yet was all about them.

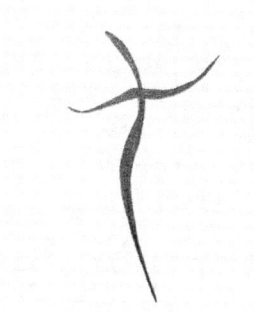

Chapter Ten

"Like I told y'all in the beginning," Sophy said, "we donkeys are called Christophore or Christ-Bearer because Jesus the Lamb rode one of our kind right after he was born and right before they put him to death."

"Was it one of them tall proud steeds? Nope. It was us lowly donks who carried God-Son through the streets, with people clothes draped on our backs."

Royce noted Chrissy's high head even though she was sitting on the ground. Part of him wanted to laugh because with her neck at that angle, she reminded him of Dara. He wouldn't say that to her, though. The other part of him was warm in the heart that she knew how special she was. It was amazing He tuned in again to Sophy.

"That parade was right before He did the most important thing of all time. Yes, sir, he received a king's greeting. He deserved it. But us donkeys? We didn't do nary a thing to put us in that position; the Awesome One picked us out special. Christophera and her filly bore the Almighty Messenger on backs straightened with gratitude, wonder, and honor. I could split a gut with pride. Yup, it was mighty special."

Sophy sat with that thought; her face was glowing in appreciation. Then her face became sober. "Now this next part is like bitter and sweet grass mixed. Soon after that, The Adored One became The Scorned, willingly. Those self-same folks who lifted Him up in honor, turned right around and lifted him up in shame. It was really their shame, not his. But he bore the burden. Now that's what y'all call Love. Even though they were fickle and treated him foul, He let them fasten him high up on a tree to die like a criminal. He wanted to give them a chance to change and be free on into the Forever.

"A lot of folks don't know this," Sophy continued after a solemn pause, "but we Christophores have cross-shaped markings on our backs. The story passed down from my kind is that it is from the shadow of the wood that lifted up God-Son to the sky. Not all shadows are bad; some shadows have light attached to them. We carried the baby to birth; we carried the man to death. Now we carry the sign of hope."

"My kind witnessed the whole caboodle -- the love and the mercy. We sho'nuff can't un-see or un-hear. And ain't no way we can keep our heehaws to ourselves 'bout that. We can't help but to keep on telling the story. And now that y'all know, y'all can add your tongues, too."

Both Royce and Chrissy looked at Sophy as if her one head had turned into three. She chuckled. "What? Did ya think I was jawing for nothing? World-Maker gave y'all some special gifts."

"But…" Royce started.

"No butts or patooties," Sophy said with a wink. "Royce, you're up for Donkey-hood. So, wiggle them ears and wag that tongue. It's a special job to bray about the good news. Folks need to be free of the things that's got a 'hold of them. They sho'nuff need mercy, so they can have some peace and joy."

Royce was thinking that he was weird enough already. What people called his gifts usually scared people and turned them away. Besides he was still just a kid.

"There's all kinds of reasons that folks give themselves for not sharing the good things they know," Sophy said. "'My tongue is too thick, I'm too young.'"

Royce flinched at that. "People say that they come from the wrong side of the tracks, they claim to be for sho' a hot mess. Hey, I'm just a dumb animal," Sophy cut her eyes at Chrissy, whose turn it was to flinch. "Somebody might chuck rocks at me, they ain't gonna listen, or my family will think I've gone bat poop crazy."

"It seems too big for me and for Chrissy," said Royce.

"Well now, you'll just have a Royce-sized job to do. And World-Maker will give you the equipment you need. You just have to call this to mind:

> *'Just keep on living like I told you to, then you'll really be my followers. You will know and understand the truth....and you can share all you've seen and heard in Jerusalem and in all Judea and Samaria and all over the earth.'*
> *'World-Maker is sending Spirit, His Helper, in My name to teach you everything, and to remind you of all the things I told you.'*

"Those are some comforting words from Jesus, the Prince of Peace and Son of God. Don't you worry none. You just have to keep your ears and heart open."

Royce wasn't sure how comforted he was. He had

already messed up with Chrissy, and he was scared he would mess up with Chadwick. But then he realized that God was already helping him. He had Sophy and he had his parents. And he had Chrissy back. It was still a bit uncomfortable with his donkey, but he believed that, hoped that, things would get back to normal. He had an inkling that normal was going to mean something else."

"I can tell that your brain is all greased up, Royce, and a lot of thoughts are sliding around in there."

Chrissy nuzzled Royce, "I already know how it feels when you don't know what to do and it seems like sunlight will never shine on your patch of grass again. Sophy is right, World-Maker sent comfort to me." Royce looked down, "I'm not trying to make you feel bad; I'm trying to cheer us both up. I think that The Mighty One always sends us help, but we don't always take it. I almost didn't listen to Sophy because my misery was like my best friend. I think if I keep that memory close, I'll have courage in other hard times."

Sophy nodded. "One of my reminders is that stamp of the cross on my back. It reminds me that my kin were Christ-Bearers, and that is my and Chrissy's legacy. But you don't have to be left out of that, Royce. You may not have a cross on your back but you can still show the marks. You probably didn't know this, but early Christ-Followers took on our name. They called themselves Christophore to show that they carried Christ in their hearts. They imitated Christ's humility, poverty, and patience. They kept the story going by love; it showed up in their words and in their service to others. World-Maker hasn't changed his stripes. He still likes to pop up in unexpected ways and places. That keeps us on our hooves. And I 'spect He likes funning us a bit.

"Will we always know who the Helper is?" Asked Royce.

"Y'all just might see Spirit if you look real close. For example, in a stovepipe hat wearer, an I-have-a-Dream dreamer, or a wee one's small voice, *those* people, *that* church, a woman living with lepers, your next-door neighbor. The Christ-Carrier might have fur and long ears. And maybe…you might see God-Son's reflection in the mirror."

"Oh," said Royce, "I hadn't thought about those people or those kinds of things being the Light. I thought it was always bigger and more complicated."

"I won't be feeding you any loco grass! At times, it does have a lot of complicated parts. But sometimes it is as simple as a smile. Just open those eyes and give your ears a wiggle. Let truth and love drown out those fake voices. Yep, people called us donkeys some foul names, and still do. But God-Son left us a more precious new name that we try to live into. Find out a new name for yourself or just take up ours. We don't mind one itty bit. Be a piece of the good news story. Looky here at this good for instance:

> *But a Samaritan, who was travelling, came upon a man who got robbed and beat up bad; and when he saw him, his heart had pity on him. He bandaged the man's wounds, pouring on oil and wine. He even put the man on his own donkey, took him to an inn and continued to take care of him.*
>
> *This is what you need to know: power will come to you when the Ruach ha-Kodesh, which is another name for Spirit, has come upon you.'*

"Those courage-giving words are from Jesus, the Light of the World."

"I'd like to try out a name besides 'weird,'" Royce said. "But if I changed my regular name now, that would seem even stranger to folks."

Sophy answered, "Other donks or humankind will call me what they want to. But even if they call me fool or make me a joke, I'll carry on. I bore up under worse; but me and my kind have also borne so much better – the Holy One. I know my true name; it's pressed into my heart.

"I'm no fool, but I'll take 'foolish.' Folks might be aiming to be mean, but my ears pick up on a different tune. Paul (that know-it-all-used-to-be-murderer-who-got-laid-low) said, 'God chose the foolish things of the world to shame the wise.' Well, I'm right happy to be of service."

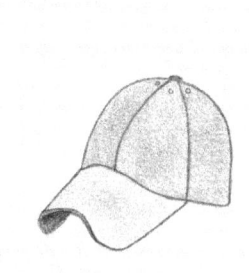

Chapter Eleven

Royce was quiet in the following days. Not a bad quiet; it was the kind that considered things and contemplated different actions. When he awakened Wednesday morning, he was nervous but resolved. He knew that he needed to do a hard thing. It was the first day back to school after the little break. It didn't seem like a little break though. The last time he'd been to school, Chad had been there with him. That was a million years ago.

The thought of Chad made his chest ache. He had so many wishes for his friend. Mother and Father taught him how to give those wishes to God. It helped.

All day, every day, he would lift up those wishes. And each day, he texted Chad long messages and received shorter and shorter replies. Royce understood. Even though he loaded on God his prayers for Chad, still, some of his scared came through. Mother said that was okay; that scared fit the situation, but to try and not let the scared take over. Royce tried.

When Royce entered the school without Chad, he was pleased that some schoolmates still smiled and said hi. He didn't know if it would be the same by the end of the day. The hard thing was coming up.

After Science class was lunchtime. Royce took slow steps to the cafeteria with his lunch pack in his hand. He searched the room until he spied the person he was looking for. He had hoped that most wouldn't notice him, but that was not the case. As he walked past the tables to the other side of the room, it seemed to him that the students were unnaturally quiet. He felt his face go warm and his fingers go cold. At last, he arrived at the person whose hunched figure flinched as if waiting for a blow. Waves of feelings drenched him. He wanted to block them and lock them away, but he let them meet his heart. Shame washed over him but was overshadowed by resolution.

"I was mean to you and I'm very sorry," Royce

said to Lyda Hoskins. "I hope you can forgive me."

Lyda looked at him with surprised and wary eyes. Royce knew she was waiting for monster words to come out of his mouth. "I'd like to sit with you if you don't mind."

Still Lyda said nothing. Royce sat and took out his thermos of beef and broccoli soup along with the other food items, and of course, the notes that Mother and Father always left. He usually hid those, but not today. There was no shame in having parents who cared.

Bit by bit, Lyda relaxed. Her body leaned more towards Royce and away from the wall. After a couple of bites of her sandwich she looked down at the table and said in a small mumble, "I'm sorry too."

Royce's heart went high. He pushed a pear and a carrot over to Lyda. She did look at him then, curiosity in her eyes. With a sideways smile, she picked up the carrot and took a big bite.

"You know, you are kind of strange," she said without any meanness attached.

"I know, and I don't mind," Royce said.

"I don't mind either," Lyda replied.

"Can I say something?" Royce asked in a more serious voice.

Lyda stiffened but nodded.

"It wasn't because of you. You didn't do anything wrong. Sometimes people are selfish." Lyda nodded after a time.

"And don't stop singing. It will help you and others. And if you need a friend, I'll be one."

"Okay."

Royce heard the tears in her voice and saw them on her face. But they were the good kind.

At the end of the school day, he had heard the word 'weird' and other unflattering names a imed at him. He was a little sad, but he knew his true name, and no one could take that away. There was something good, too. Several kids said, "Goodbye, Royce. See you tomorrow."

* * *

A few weeks later came a surprise. It was a sur-prise that would test the new knowledge and decisions of Royce's and Chrissy's hearts. On a particular day, the two donkeys and the boy returned from the meadow after a short stay. The chilled air did not favor boys with-out a coat of fur.

Suddenly, Royce let out a gasp of joy and took off running towards the front of his house. Sophy hurried after him and so did Chrissy. A car was there, causing Chrissy's heart to beat faster and a knot to form in her belly. The passenger door opened and out came someone familiar and strange. Royce embraced Chad with gentle exuberance, and he was embraced in turn.

A sour green feeling settled over Chrissy. Chad was back and he was even uglier, she thought. She realized that the strangeness was because Chad's face had no hair, no brows or lashes. And when his cap was knocked off by the mutual hugs, she saw that there was none atop his head either. How could Royce want to spend time with that? Fear got a grip on her too. What if he dumped her again? That hurt had been bad and was mending, but what if Chad stole him away like before?

Then Chad's eyes, big and dark, fastened on hers. They took each other in. Royce turned in the direction of Chad's eyes and quickly released his friend, who immediately swayed on those spindly legs of his that were even thinner now. Chrissy remembered thinking they were elegant when he'd first appeared, but now they looked awkward like a fawn just beginning to walk. As Chrissy had feared, Royce turned away from her, his arms circling Chad's shoulders. It was too much for her; she turned her back and headed for the barn. She was hurt and angry in turn.

"Well, what's got your britches in a swivel?" asked Sophy, startling Chrissy. She had forgotten about the other donk.

"I told you he would hurt me again," she spat out.

"How has he hurt you?" asked Sophy.

"You saw him; he chose Chad again." Chrissy was walking around the yard in an agitated way. Sophy was keeping up.

"I saw him greet a friend who has been gone a long time."

"Exactly."

"I still don't see how that is hurting you," Sophy said.

"He's my boy!"

"Oh, I see. You want him all to yourself."

Chrissy stopped pacing around and glared at Sophy. "You know what I mean. Chad is the one who made Royce act bad with me."

"You mean he crawled up inside Royce's brain and took over his mind?"

Chrissy flounced off in exasperation, but Sophy stayed with her. "Go away, I want to be alone."

"Nope. Not gonna do it. Haven't you been listening to anything I said?"

"Of course, your story made Royce see the light and come back to me."

"Stop being a dunderhead! Those stories were

for you too. Royce does not belong to just you. He's special; the world needs him. You are jealous. And jealousy is the kind of thing that separates people. It'll be your fault this time unless you get a hold of yourself."

"But you saw the way Chad looked at me. He doesn't want Royce with me. Why don't you talk to him?"

"Royce isn't your and Chad's personal wishbone. Stop poor mouthing about yourself long enough to think about someone else. Your fur ain't exactly clean. How do you think Royce feels being pulled like that? Do you even care? Are you really his friend if you just want to do what you claim Chad did? Is your head stuck that far up your tookus? If you're gonna web up in feeling sorry for yourself, maybe I spent worthless time on you. I pegged you for special too. But I see you're wasting your gift on selfishness." Sophy turned her back and started for the barn.

Chrissy was stunned quiet for a while, but then called to Sophy, "Wait." She dipped her nose, "You're right. I guess I was just scared. I wasn't thinking of Royce."

"Do you believe he was sincere when he apologized?"

"I know he was," said Chrissy. "I guess I just

thought that it would mean that he would dump Chad."

"I want you to chew on this, young donk. You know that Royce has gifts, and you know that it has to do with being a light bearer. So, if he is spending some of his heart on Chad, there must be a reason." She waited.

Chrissy merely frowned. Sophy rolled her eyes and sighed.

"Let go of your anger and self-focus and think on why Chad is like he is. Be a Light-Bearer."

Chrissy truly wanted to see what all the fuss over Chad was. She lay down on the ground and looked at images in her head. She asked World-Maker for help. Then she let out a gasp. How had she missed it? She knew how... Not all was her fault, but her jealousy had gotten in the way.

"There is wrongness in his body," she said, allowing herself to feel compassion for him.

"Yes," said Sophy.

"Is he close to going to Forever?"

"That's not for me to say, but it is a lot to take on for those who haven't been on this round ball very long. How do you know that you aren't here for such a time as this?"

"Royce needs me." Chrissy felt as if her vision was clearing. Her heart was clearing too. She had been looking at things in a small way. Things were bigger than her hurt.

"And open your heart to Chadwick needing you, too," Sophy admonished.

Chrissy was skeptical about that part, but she nodded. At the very least, if Chad needed Royce, then Chrissy could be there for Royce, no matter what. She had a feeling she would soon find out what that meant.

Chapter Twelve

The knots and tightness gripping Royce's shoulders and belly relaxed in relief. It was the day after Chad's return and he was in the barn with Chrissy. Sophy wasn't around. He had just informed his donkey that he would be spending time each day at Chad's.

"I understand," said Chrissy. "Chad needs you. I'll be here. My back is strong and my heart is getting wider; you may lean and rest when you need to."

"Oh, Chrissy," Royce uttered with a choke in his voice. He took that moment to indeed lean and rest for some moments, gathering comfort and courage.

Fear had sat on his head earlier. He'd been afraid

that Chrissy would be hurt again, and that was nearly unbearable to him. He'd imagined himself like a fraying rope being pulled from both ends. He was determined to do his best to be a friend and light-bearer to both, but Chrissy's response meant that he wouldn't have a trembling heart -- at least, not where she was concerned. Chad was a different matter.

Royce had sensed Chad's fear mixed with his happiness to see him. He would try to explain, to help him see like Sophy had helped him. He hoped that Chad would understand. In the meantime, he left Chrissy in the barn and set his feet to go to Father's bench. It was Father's private place in the opposite direction from Royce's meadow. Father went there to talk and listen to God. Royce rarely disturbed him there, but knew that Father would welcome him if he showed up. He could also use human arms to lean into.

Royce made his way in an unhurried walk, buttoning his jacket against the sharp breeze. He noticed that the trees only had a sparse amount of leaves clinging to them. Before long they would give up their position, making room for the trees' next temporary residents.

He was still a-ways from the bench when he saw Father. The thinned foliage made it possible to see what he couldn't when it was full and lush. What he saw halted his steps. Father sat on his bench with his face buried against the fur of Sophy's neck.

Royce observed the tender exchange. He could feel a strong, old connection between the two. He was surprised and wondered why he had not noticed before. He watched as the man and donkey talked and laughed; he felt the taste of the sweet and bitter berries.

The sight was a wonder to Royce. Some understanding came over him, but also a million questions. He didn't ask them or move closer. Instead, he turned his steps back to leave the two with their moments.

Later, while supping with his father, just the two of them because mother was out with her friends, he asked a question.

"Is Sophy your donkey, Father?"

"Yes. But not just mine anymore." Father looked steadily at Royce, and Royce saw the deepness of his feelings.

"Is it hard, Poppy?" Royce asked, gently using his little boy word for his father.

"Yes. But it's good to see her now."

"Will she come back again?" asked Royce, hoping for his father's sake that she would.

Father was quiet for a beat, "I don't know, son. This was a special visit."

"Do a lot of people have donkeys who talk?"

"No, Royce. It's very rare. They help in certain situations."

"Father, are you weird like me?"

Father chuckled, "No, I'm weird like me."

Royce laughed too. "But how come you had a donkey?"

"Sophy prepared me to raise someone special and help prepare him for light-bearing."

That boggled Royce's mind, causing his brow to wrinkle. "So, you knew about me before I was born?"

"Sort of. As you know, when I met your mother, she was already carrying you, but I didn't know it. When I found out, I loved you before you were born; and as I've said before, I loved you even more when I met you."

"Yes, I know Father," Royce said with surety. There was nary a pinch of doubt about that. "But, when did you know that I was the one that you had to prepare special?"

"Well, I had my suspicions when you seemed to sense what others were feeling. And later, when you began to talk, revealing that you truly did know things, then, I was pretty sure. But when Chrissy was born, and you knew her name, I was certain."

Royce looked at his dad, searching his eyes. He had a harder time feeling his father and now he thought he knew why. He hadn't needed to know about being a messenger too soon. It would have been too much for his shoulders.

"But Father, do you mind terribly. Was there something else you wanted to do? He was remembering a time when Father would go off to work like Mother. Royce vaguely remembered that it had to do with being a boss for a magazine. It wasn't something that passed through his mind often. But in this moment, guilt rose up in him. Nowadays, his father wrote some articles, but mostly he took care of the house, the few animals, the garden, and of course, Royce."

"I did, but being with your mother and being here for you gives me seven times more joy than that."

"I'm sorry, Father. "

"I'm not sorry, son."

They sat without talking. Royce was able to feel his Father's feelings for a bit and it made his heart swell. That's how he knew.

"Father. Sophy is leaving soon, isn't she?"

"Yes. On Sunday. I'll take her to a special place."

"I'll go with you, and you can hold my hand."

"I'd like that."

"Poppy?"

"What is it, my treasure?"

"I love you."

Chapter Thirteen

It felt too soon for Chrissy. She wasn't ready for Sophy to leave her. In her mind pictures, she saw them being companions at least through Spring. She hadn't fooled herself that Sophy would stay forever; she knew that there were others that needed a donkey of Sophy's sort.

"But what about Chad and Royce. There's so much to be done here," she pleaded with the older donk.

"That's your own carrot patch to tend, Chrissy. You'll do a dandy job. Just recall the words I said. And most of all, remember that World-Maker really is the Mighty One. You won't be by yourself."

Chrissy made her face long, "Why does everybody leave me?"

"Now don't be dipping in the pity pot. It will pull you in and stew you up in its juices. You'll likely not have an easy time getting shed of it."

"But…"

"None of them buts. Self-pity is a trap that has your name on it. Beware, especially because that's a fig leaf you like to wear."

Chrissy was about to protest that it wasn't her fault that people treated her mean and why was she always getting the blame for someone else's doings. But she caught herself and dropped her head, sheepishly avoiding Sophy's knowing look.

"I'll miss you," she said simply.

"I'll miss you too, young donk. I'm right proud of you. I can see why you were chosen. Some troublesome times will come; but the mark on your back is a reminder of your sacred duty to bear the light. You are equipped."

At Sophy's words, Chrissy lifted her head and straightened her back. Even though Sophy was giving her a mixed barrel of berries, she would do her best to see it not as a punishment, but as a privilege.

"That's my girl, Chrissy," Sophy said. "Now, let's go to our favorite place in the meadow. While I'm still here is not the time for droopy ears."

***

Royce could tell that Chad wanted to believe him. But there were so many weeds in his mind tripping him up. He was at his friend's house, having brought schoolwork and was helping him with it. He'd told Chad some things about the talking donkeys and light-bearing. He started out nervous but had ended up pushing his words out like rapids over stones.

With a big frown, Chad said, "I heard my dad say that there is no God, but if there is, He's evil." He looked at Royce in a challenging and hopeful way.

"But he's wrong," Royce started, then immediately saw that his words did the opposite of what he wanted. He could tell that it made Chad feel emptier and more insecure. He tried explaining things like Sophy had, but it confused his friend. Royce's shoulders sagged.

"It's okay," Chad said sadly. "I know you want me to feel better. I do feel better with you here." A familiar anxious expression settled on his face. "Can you stay a little while longer? We can play Rummikub."

"Yes, I will." Royce was disappointed with himself. But at least he could play a game. He set up the card table and game in front of the soft chair that Chad rested in. He pulled up a chair from the desk. It jerked his heart to see the effort it took for Chad to place his tiles on his rack. He didn't comment or try to help his friend, knowing that would add to Chad's sorrow.

Five minutes after they finally started, their mothers came in to say that Chad needed to rest, and Royce needed to get home to feed the donkeys. Royce felt Chad's panic at the mention of the donkeys.

"You'll come tomorrow, won't you?" he asked Royce, his eyes big and round, filled with the ever-present fear.

Royce hesitated, "I can't tomorrow. I'm going with Father to take Sophy somewhere. But I'll be back Sunday afternoon. We can visit and play then." He watched his friend and felt the shuttering of his heart.

"Sure," said Chad, "I'm tired now. Good-bye."

He got into his bed aided by his mother, turning his face to the wall. Royce stood helpless until his Mother's hands guided him out. When they were in the car, she said, "Sometimes people have to fight their battles alone inside themselves. And our only job is to walk beside them and offer our ears and our arms."

"I wish I could make him understand. But I keep doing things wrong. I don't know what to do."

"God knows exactly what Chad needs. Why don't we talk to Him about it?"

Royce smiled in sheepish relief, "That's a good idea. Sometimes I forget I'm not Him."

Chapter Fourteen

Early Saturday morning Father and Royce loaded Sophy into a special trailer. The sun was just making its rounds, poking though convenient holes in the fog, finally taking it over. Royce felt special traveling beside his father. Mother had packed some snacks and treats for her men and Sophy. She'd also given Royce a note just for him. After several rounds of goodbyes, kisses and hugs, she released them. Royce watched her wave until he could no longer see her.

It was a long drive. They stopped various times to give their legs a stretch and to do necessary human and animal things. Royce didn't know where they were going. Father simply said, "You'll see."

It was mostly a quiet ride, because some out loud words didn't need to be said. Royce tried to memorize everything he saw in case he had to travel that way again. It kind of felt like he would not see Sophy again, but one never knew. And maybe he would have to make this trip in the future for a reason he didn't want to think much about.

They still hadn't arrived when the moon appeared, taking over for the sun. Father turned onto what was hardly a road at all. Royce would have passed right by it. The area was thick with trees and brush. After a while of bouncing along in the increasing darkness and unrelieved forest, Royce started to wonder if maybe they'd made a wrong turn. Gripping tightly to the seat, he peered at Father and saw that his face was calm. Father, not taking his eyes off the dim path, spoke,

"Hang on, it's not much further."

Royce did hang on. Finally, the bumps smoothed out and he could see brightness in the near distance. Suddenly they drove into a clearing where a wooden, well-lit house sat. A tall man stood on the porch leaning against a post at the top of the stairs. Father gave a toot and the man lifted his hand in greeting. He moved towards them as Father stopped the truck.

"Are we leaving Sophy here, Father?" Royce asked. He uncurled his fingers and flexed his knuckles.

"No, we're going to stay here overnight with my friend."

The tall man reached the truck as Father got out.

"Ellis," Father said.

"John," the man said.

They only said those words, but Royce could hear miles and years, and a language of respect and caring that had deep, entwined roots. He watched, remaining in the passenger seat as the two men did a hand grip shoulder pat embrace. Then the man whom Father had called Ellis turned his eyes to Royce.

"Come on out and meet Mr. Ellis," Father said.

Royce opened the door, planning to join the two on the other side, but Ellis took long, quick strides to where Royce was. Father followed.

"Welcome, traveler," Mr. Ellis said with warm sincerity. "I'm honored to meet you, Royce." He held out his hand.

Royce took the hand that swallowed his. Mr. Ellis reminded him of a tree. His dark skin had a reminiscence of wind and sun etched there. Royce could tell he was old, but he seemed strong and solid.

"Nice to meet you," he replied.

Mr. Ellis clapped him on the back with a hardiness that matched his size. Royce was proud that he kept his footing.

"Come on in and get some eats," Mr. Ellis said. "And I'll show you where you'll be bunking."

Royce looked at his father, slightly nervous.

"Go on, I'll take care of Sophy and be right in."

Royce followed Mr. Ellis in and any trepidation he'd had was forgotten when he walked into the house. The large, open space with cathedral ceilings certainly called to his attention, but the aromas coming from a table laden with food grabbed Royce by the nose, pulling him in that direction. His stomach gave a resounding rumble of appreciation.

Before long, Royce was settled with a heaping plate of vegetables and meats and cornbread. He had his eye on the desserts, trying to decide between apple crumble and chocolate cake. Father joined them, and he and Mr. Ellis spoke of people that Royce didn't know. He didn't mind not being included. He liked seeing his father with that relaxed look on his face, laughing and talking with someone who'd known him before Royce was born. It seemed lately he was seeing his father as a person and not just as his dad. It was interesting.

He didn't have to choose desserts because Mr.

Ellis gave him heaping helpings of both, the remnants of which he swiped clean with his finger. Royce marveled that he did not feel too full. Soon after, his father rescued his head from hitting the table and suggested that he turn in. Royce was too sleepy for embarrassment, recalling only the murmur of voices as slumber ushered in, until the pale rays of sun gently nudged him into a new day.

They ate big, fluffy waffles with the perfect amount of crunch, topped with whipped cream and maple syrup. Again, he ate more that he thought he had room for, without getting a bad stomach.

When it was time to leave, Father got Sophy settled back in the trailer. Mr. Ellis laid one hand on Royce's head and the other on his shoulder. "It's a happy man that can accept the boots made for his feet." Royce nodded solemnly, not totally understanding, but knowing it was important.

Father and Mr. Ellis repeated their greeting ritual but with a longer embrace. Mr. Ellis called out 'God speed' as they pulled away. Royce took up his task of hanging onto the seat as they traversed the rough terrain.

When the road was smoother, Royce again attempted to memorize the route. It was with dismay that he found himself waking up. They'd also stopped, apparently having reached their destination.

"We're here," Father said.

Royce hadn't even remembered being drowsy. He rubbed his eyes and stretched. Looking around, he caught his breath. There were no words for what he saw. Father laughed at his goggle-eyed perusal of the surroundings.

"Oh, Poppy," he said after moments of staring in awe.

"I know," said Father.

The two of them got out and opened the trailer for Sophy.

"Ahh," breathed Sophy, as if returning to an old friend. She stood taking in the wondrous sight with an expression of anticipation touched by sorrow.

"It's been a real pleasure to know you, spawn of Johnny," Sophy finally said to Royce. She leaned her neck for a hug and a nuzzle which Royce gave her, clinging as he uttered thank you's.

"Shucks," Sophy said after he had straightened up, "I wouldn't have been there if you weren't ready. Now you make sure you and Chrissy lift each other's arms and hooves. Y'all need each other to grow up straight. Chrissy is right handy to have around because you never know when you might happen across a road

angel. And if you do, don't go beating on your donkey."
She gave Royce a wink.

Sophy looked over at Father. Royce saw Father's
chest rise and fall from the deep breaths he was taking.
Sophy pawed at the ground, looking down at it.

"I'll wait in the truck for you, Father," Royce
said. His father nodded. He and Sophy walked slowly
towards a path that Royce was pretty sure was not there
a second before.

Royce watched as his father got down on his
knees when they reached the entrance to the path. Man
and donkey said goodbye. The tenderness, sadness, and
love were sharp and clear, reaching Royce's heart, causing
his eyes to sting and brim. After a long bit, Royce cleared
the moisture from his eyes with a swipe of his hand. He
blinked. The path was gone and so was Sophy. Only Father stood where Sophy once was. His Adam's apple was
bobbing, and tears were escaping down his cheeks.

Royce climbed out of the truck, went to his Father, and tucked his hand into the bigger one, squeezing
tight. Father squeezed back.

On the way home, Royce fell asleep again. There
was no dismay this time. He understood some things
that caused awe in his heart; things which he knew he
could not utter even if he had the words. When they

were miles away or worlds away, whichever, he remembered the note from mother. He took it out.

"Poppy, Mother says we are to stop at Bridges Soda Shop and you are to have a banana milkshake and curly fries."

Father grinned. "Well, if she says we need to do that, then we must obey. Just wait until you taste their banana shakes, son of mine. They are almost like magic; they make people feel better."

"I can tell that the magic has already started," Royce grinned too.

Chapter Fifteen

Chrissy was alone in the meadow enjoying the throwback warmth of the sun. The weather had a suggestion of summer but carried a sharper edge. When the shadow of the boy stole into the sunlight, she wasn't surprised; still she shivered.

Chad stood looking at her, the tang of his emotions stinging her nose. Chrissy wondered how the boy had managed to walk that far. His trousers were flapping on legs that were like delicate tree saplings. His arms were a match. Instinctively, she moved closer, sensing his need for support.

Chad scrambled back, swaying a little. Resentment surged from him in erratic waves, the power of which appeared to lend him energy. Chrissy stopped her advance. Compassion flooded her being even as fear threatened to block it. She watched as Chad bent to pick up a stone and heave it towards her. She let out an involuntary cry as it made contact with her flank, breaking through her coat and skin. She could feel her blood mingling with her hair.

Her hooves were itching to speed her away from the whirling currents that had possession of Chad. But Chrissy kept her ground, recalling the cross mark on her back. And she remembered her true name.

Chad continued to throw rocks and words like arrows that pierced her heart. Chrissy marveled at the courage that compelled her to move closer to the boy.

"I'm not your enemy, Chad," she said.

Chad's eyes widened upon hearing human words from Chrissy. Still, he picked up more stones and tossed them at Chrissy. Some hit their mark, but most were ineffectual as the temporary strength of Chad's anger leached away.

"I need Royce to be my friend. But you keep getting in the way. I need him more than you do." Chad aimed a weak kick at Chrissy that just skimmed her foreleg. He was fighting to keep on his feet; the color had fled his skin.

"He is your friend, Chad." Chrissy moved even closer. "You have me, too. I know I never said sorry to you. You tried to be my friend with the pears. I didn't let you. I'll let you now. Here; lean on me. I have a strong back. I can help carry you."

He saw that Chad tried to keep standing, but his legs betrayed, refusing to aid him in remaining upright. They folded, causing the rest of him to follow. Chrissy quickly caught his fall, guiding him down with her body. Chad had no choice but to rest against her, tremulous and weak. Chrissy uttered soothing sounds.

"I'm going to be all alone. It'll probably be dark," Chad said at last, his voice thin and despairing. Royce makes me feel like I had somebody, not so alone. But soon I'll be by myself. I'm so scared, Chrissy. I'm scared. I'm so scared. Royce said that God made a Forever that has light and beautiful things. But my dad says there is no such thing as a good God because He made me sick. My dad is smart and a grown-up and right about a lot of things. I want there to be a Forever, but I'm scared that my dad is right. I'm sick of scared. It won't even leave me alone in my dreams."

Chad started weeping piteously, his tears wetting Chrissy's coat. He clung there, sobbing sorry and sorrow into her fur. The tears mingled with the blood, mixing into her wounds, making them smart.

Chrissy positioned herself to nuzzle Chad's neck. "There is a Forever, Chad, I promise you." She felt Chad's arm reach her neck to cling feebly there.

"I want to believe it, Chrissy, so bad. Maybe Dad will love me again and not turn away when he looks at me. Maybe he'll stay home more and be with me." He lifted his head and looked at Chrissy, a pleading hope in his eyes.

Chrissy's heart felt torn up for Chad. The boy had a heavy load to carry, and he didn't have her strong back. Guilt sliced through her and threatened to take over her heart, but she knew that way was folly. Chagrined, she knew that self-pity would follow close behind if she became self-focused. But Chrissy didn't know what to do. Chad was waiting for her to help him and she wanted to so badly. Then it occurred to her that she wasn't the Mighty One, but she could ask Him for help.

From almost the moment that she lifted her pleas to World-Maker, Chrissy felt as if she had new eyes. It was weird. She didn't know how to explain it or what it meant. Then, she did.

"Look," she said with reverence, pointing behind Chad. Chad sat up and slowly turned to where Chrissy's eyes directed. His mouth hung open and not a sound came out; not even a gasp. Chrissy saw his skin reflect colors, some of which she'd not seen before.

"Those are your angels," Chrissy said of the host standing there. It was hard to tell if they were near or far. They were there. Words of Truth came off Chrissy's tongue, "They have always been near you and will continue to be. And when it's time for you to enter Forever, they will be with you, lighting the way, holding your hand. You will not be alone."

Both Chrissy and Chad gazed in wonder at the glorious beings that appeared young and ancient, mighty and tender; neither male nor female. Boy nor donkey could mark the moment when the sight of them went away. The glory of their presence remained long after the two recognized that they could no longer see them. Their peace stayed as well, wrapping around them, cushioning them like a bed of goose feathers.

Chrissy noticed that at some point Chad had entangled his fingers in her fur, giving little strokes. When their vision had returned to almost normal, Chad said, "I hurt you, Chrissy. I'm sorry."

"I forgive you, Chad."

"Thank you. I can't take it all back, but let me wash your wounds now, please."

Chrissy hesitated because Chad was so weak. She knew however, that the boy, sick as he was, needed to act out his sorry.

And so, he did. Chrissy stood still, letting Chad clean up the mess of her fur with his socks and the water from the nearby creek. Though it hurt, it was a wondrous hurt. They had a new understanding that spoke in the still of silence, the gentle washing of fur. There was peace between them and a bond of experience that was just theirs. Chrissy knew what it cost Chad to give his limited energy to taking care of the hurts that he had inflicted. She didn't take that away from him. She did offer her neck for his cheek to rest upon after he was done. And Chad accepted, sinking into the fur gratefully. That was how Royce found them.

Chapter Sixteen

When Royce got home and found that Chad was not in Royce's room as the two tea drinking mothers had said, his heart sped up in panic. He raced to the barn and then to the meadow. At first, the stillness of Chad lying there reduced the speed of his heart, almost stopping it. As he got closer, Chrissy lifted her head, which also roused Chad. Royce let his breath escape.

His relief was soon followed by dismay as he took in the damage to Chrissy's coat, and the bloody socks. Just before his dismay turned into rage, Chrissy quickly jumped up and moved in front of Chad.

"All is good, Royce, everything is good. Something amazing happened." Royce listened as Chrissy told the story. Chad quietly added a few things, intently watching Royce's face, dipping his head in shame several times.

By and by, Royce let his shoulders relax and his hands unfurl. He marveled at the way Chrissy nuzzled Chad occasionally and allowed him to lean on her. A thick, green feeling wanted him to snatch away his friend's hand from his donkey's fur. He was tempted to take away the comfort of that gesture and proclaim, "She's my donkey." The memory of Father and Sophy intervened. He wanted to be as brave as his father. Chrissy didn't belong to just him. Her heart was big enough for more. A quick wink from Chrissy made the sludgy green recede even more. It wasn't gone, Royce knew, but was waiting for another opportunity. He would have to stay alert.

"I'm sorry," Chad was saying. "I wouldn't blame you if you don't want to be my friend anymore, Royce. I kinda get it now. I've been so scared all the time. I hated feeling like that. I felt better around you. But it wasn't enough. I put the blame on Chrissy because I was jealous. I didn't know what to do, so I made you choose me. I was a jerk." He sunk his head low.

Royce squirmed. He knew all about being mean.

He looked at Chrissy who had forgiven him. "But I didn't have to listen, Chad. He went over and sat beside Chad, draping an arm across his shoulders, "Of course, I'm still your friend. I'm happy that you saw the angels."

Chad gave a beatific smile. "Thank you, Royce. Now I know there really is a Forever, and I'm not so scared. I can't wait to tell my Dad. Maybe he won't be so mad at me."

"He's not mad at you, Chad." Royce said. "He's just really sad that you're sick, and it makes him mad that his money can't fix you. When he looks at you, he only sees that he failed to make you get better."

"But do you think that if he knows that we can be in the Forever together, he'll look at me like he used to, like he was happy to see me?"

"I hope so," said Royce.

"But if you go, his heart will be torn up with missing you on this side of Forever," Chrissy added. "Longing for those you care about, and being sad when you can't see them, is another side of love."

"But he's missing me now, while I'm still here," Chad said.

"Tell him about the angels. And tell him you be lieve, and ask him to play Rummikub with you," Royce said.

"I will," promised Chad. "I hope I have time to play many games with him, and with you, Royce." He looked at Chrissy shyly, "And you, too."

"That will be just dandy," Chrissy said, reminding herself of Sophy. "And our hearts will tear when you are missing," Chrissy said. Royce nodded.

* * *

Royce and Chrissy were never the same way they used to be. Their experiences had made them different. With more gnarls in their roots and branches, but still intertwined, their bond more secure. The new thing that sprang up was made of both light and shadows, clearly seen, and somehow stronger in its honesty. There was no path back, only forward. Where once their roots had crowded each other, now there was space for new growth.

In the meantime, they savored their togetherness. They still enjoyed frolicking sunshine moments, more precious now because of growing up things. They kept company with frogs and other creatures of nature. Their fascination went beyond the shape of stones and the sunlight upon winged creatures, expanding to encompass deeper things.

Their meadow moments were often shared with Chad, at least, when he wasn't spending time with his dad who wasn't mad any more. In later times, Lyda Hoskins joined them, after which Royce would pretend not to see the smirk on Chrissy's face.

The sweetness and tartness of berries overlaid those moments. Those times were cherished because one day Royce and Chrissy's light-bearing would send them on separate roads. But the boy and the donkey were blessed to be together a goodly while; long after the angels carried Chad away.

The End

Discussion Questions

1. What did you enjoy about the book?
2. Which character(s) can you most relate to?
3. Who is your favorite character? Why?
4. Have you ever been hurt by a friend?
5. Have you ever hurt a friend?
6. Are there people different from you that make you feel uncomfortable?
7. Has anyone ridiculed you for being different?
8. Have you made fun of anyone for being different?
9. What did the book teach you about people who are different?
10. What did you learn about being a friend?
11. What are some things you learned about donkeys?
12. Have you been tempted to get back at someone who wronged you?
13. Did you get an idea of what God feels about "weird" folks?
14. What would you think of someone who walked in today dressed in animal skins and eating honey-dipped locusts?
15. Do you think Jesus was weird to some folks?

16. Which character would you most like to meet?
17. What feelings did this book bring out?
18. What did you think of the title?
19. What inspired you?
20. Is there anything you would change about yourself after reading?
21. Do you feel differently about donkeys?

Add your own questions!

About the Author

Elaine Watkins was born and raised in Georgia. Following short residences in Maryland and San Fransisco, she landed in Massachusetts. Her favorite occupations include graphic artist, nanny, and wedding cake baker. Now, a licensed mental health/pastoral counselor, she listens to heart-stories for a living. In the between times, if she is not reading or beating her friends in Rummikub, you'll find her in her writing loft. She was awarded a top prize for her essay, *The Born. On The Backs of Donkeys* is her first Middle Grade novel.